CALLIOPE

SPEED DATING WITH THE DENIZENS OF THE UNDERWORLD

BOOK FORTY

ARIEL DAWN

NAUGHTY NIGHTS PRESS LLC• CANADA

CHAPTER ONE

THE POTENT SCENT of burned sandalwood and jasmine filled the air, along with the sounds of Rick Astley's *Never Gonna Give You Up,* and Calliope sighed in earnest as she sipped her pomegranate martini.

"Try not to look so excited," Hattie—also known as Hathor, the Egyptian goddess of love, music, and beauty, and Calliope's closest friend—said with a hefty sigh. Calliope licked the tart liquid off of her lips, relishing in the bitterness of the alcohol, her nerves starting to settle barely a fraction.

Ever since Hades took over the financial adjustments, it seems the martinis are not hitting quite as hard as they used to...

"Forgive me, but I find it hard to appear excited when I am at my wit's end," Calliope mused dramatically.

Hattie shifted in her chair, adjusting the neckline of her dress—if one could call the amalgamation of linens and gold a dress with how little it actually covered the woman.

"I would think a woman such as yourself would be dying to eat up the mortals in this place," she said, raising a brow at her friend.

Calliope shrugged, rolling her amber

eyes at her friend from behind her bronze roman mask.

"The only thing I am dying to do, Hattie, is paint," she said wistfully as she drained the last bit of her martini. She slowly shook the glass in the air, trying to signal the bartender, who, it seemed, did not see her.

It used to be quite different for her. Once upon a glorious moon, Calliope truly felt as if she had it all. There was a plethora of men—and women—for a muse to inspire. Playwrights and poets searching for their spark or that one piece that would make them renowned. Musicians seeking their big break or their next record-shattering hit. Artisans dying for a drop of inspiration so they could feel the high of notoriety, so they could feel *something.* And Calliope was always there to answer the call. As a muse, it was her destiny to inspire, and in turn, the benefits sated her in a way nothing else could. As they chased their muse, the muse chased the best feeling in the world. To be adored. Worshipped. And that itself, was the highest form of inspiration a muse could discern. The praise of those Calliope serviced or took under her wing fed her like blood feeds a vampire.

Although it seems nowadays, perhaps there are other things that could feed a vampire...

Calliope pushed the thought from her mind. She did not want to think about her vampiric student, Izzy, who had somehow found her mate—in this very establishment, no less—in a shy, sweet hellhound shifter with godly connections. Not that Calliope disliked the gods and goddesses, but her relationship to those who sat on their high thrones, with statues and monuments built for them, tended to be, in Calliope's opinion, a bit full of themselves. And most gods and goddesses did not see her as an equal figure of adoration. She was a *muse.* Nothing more, nothing less. An immortal divine being meant to provide a service or gifts, rather than to be worshipped or praised.

Most gods and goddesses favored this opinion of Calliope, but Hathor and Athena considered her a friend, as well as Athena's brother, Mars—who, after his near death experience seemed all too happy these days with Lorelai, her former student and friend. And of course, there was her cocky ex-lover, Chuck—as Pegasus referred to himself nowadays. While Calliope didn't mind a good hook up once in a while, she knew better than to take up with a former flame. Especially one as self-centered as Chuck. She'd had more than her fill of his cock years ago when they were young, and though the sex was enjoyable enough, the art it produced for her was lackluster and downright embarrassing. She was rather glad when the paintings burned along with his temple.

The winged pegacorn shifter was *not* a clear path to inspiration, even albeit a temporary one for the muse. No matter how lonely she got.

But Calliope knew *something* needed to change. Her canvas had been blank for far too long. Longer than usual, due to the fact that she had not found it within herself to seek a new patron after David had...

She sighed, not wanting to think about the man. Every time she did, all she felt was remorse, pain. Guilt. And while those things could be inspiring to Calliope, they were the opposite now. She was *blocked*. Creatively, personally. Sexually. It was as frustrating as it was aggravating.

She was itching to paint, to create, but every time she stepped in front of her canvas, every time she tried to do *something*, nothing happened. Her mind was suddenly blank. It seemed quite ironic that a woman who taught painting Monday through Friday at the University of Southern California could not, in all actuality, find the muse within herself to paint. It was like a terrible joke, one that did not leave Calliope laughing.

First Mars loses his powers, and then David dies and my inspiration takes a bloody vacay without my consent...

Though in the case of Mars's lost powers, he had revived them. With his divined mate's declaration of love, of course, which gave him the *will to live.*

Ryza was always the most dramatic Fate.

Even Izzy, her former student, had found solace with her hellhound mate, saving *him* from certain death when she'd bonded him. And the two of them seemed positively enamored with one another now, which would be much more adorable if they could keep their hands off one another when they were working. At the gallery on campus Calliope now oversaw most of the time, with its owner, Professor Leehan, quietly transitioning into retirement while his son, Brian, transitioned to take his place.

But Calliope would not be able to divine anything from David Green, like Mars or Isabelle. Because David was dead. Which was her fault, clearly. After all, it was her gifts that drove him to the brink of madness before he took his own life.

Which was entirely the reason Calliope had let Hattie talk her into coming to this dreadful *speed dating* special event at Aphrodite and Eve's DeLux Cafe.

Masquerade of Mystery, a one night only special event held at the luminous cafe where the mortals and supernaturals as well as the immortals like herself could partake in a more *intimate* setting than the typical Speed Dating sessions on Wednesday nights.

It had been Hattie's idea, of course. The woman ravished impulsivity, and her idea of entertainment could often be as whimsical as her inspirations themselves. As a goddess of music and a patron of the arts, Calliope had garnered the idea sounded logical in theory—a little anonymity in an intimate, sensual setting, one that was not full of haunting memories, like the *Den of Sin,* could lead her to someone... even if it was just for a night. And knowing how many gods, goddesses, and supernaturals alike had found their mates within the DeLux Cafe, a part of her dared to hope that attending would bring her the same success. Even if it was just for one night. One night, one kiss, one spark was all Calliope truly needed, but now that she was here, in the DeLux Café, in her too-flowing silk toga with her bronzed mask and her dark hair piled atop her head, heart beating in her chest as she signaled once more for the bloody bartender, she wondered if she'd made a mistake.

What am I even doing here, truly...

"Oh, stop being such a square, Callie." Hattie dismissed her with a wave as she drained her martini.

Callie sighed once more as Hattie motioned for the bartender to bring them a fresh round of drinks. She sighed in defeat as the bartender smirked and nodded at them as someone announced that the first round of the speed date would take place in twenty minutes.

"I am not a square. I am a circle of infinite inspiration," she drawled as the bartender set a fresh pomegranate martini in front of her. Calliope did not think twice about grabbing the drink her friend had bought her, and taking a long steady sip. It was rather tart for her taste, but not bad.

Hattie chuckled beside her. "Then start acting like it, woman!" She smirked at her as she raised her glass. The goddess's bright blue eyes glowed behind her petinae'd mask, the vibrant blue streaks and feathers in her hair shimmering beneath the light. "Quit pining over how *uninspired you are* and get your butt out there in the real world again."

She glanced around the room at the men and women still pouring in, her blood chilling when she laid her eyes on a man she'd recognize anywhere. With or without a mask.

For starters, he couldn't help but make himself obvious, drawing attention wherever he went, and tonight was no exception, it seemed. His ivory suit and mask were sharp and regal, and all the gold accents—from his chain to his cufflinks to his gilded mask—were so on the nose, Callie wanted to roll her eyes.

Even if he *did* look appealing dressed like a bloody angel, complete with a set of white feathered wings.

But Pegasus was no angel. Far from it. What he was, was annoying as hell. Pretty, but annoying.

"Does he ever stay home like a

normal god?" Calliope mused aloud.

Hattie laughed. "Who? Chucky Doll? Are you serious?"

"Dead," Calliope murmured, sipping her martini. The tartness made her pucker her lips.

"I mean, can you blame the guy? His partner in crime's all settled down now, which I still can't believe *Mars* of all people could ever settle down, period, let alone with a human mate..."

Calliope chewed her lips in annoyance, and that was the moment Chuck met her gaze. He smiled his perfect toothpaste commercial smile and waved at her. She gave him a smile that was not quite genuine, clearly annoyed that she couldn't even come to the DeLux Cafe without running into someone she knew, apparently.

Is the world really that small?

She looked away dismissively, returning her attention to her friend who was tsking her.

"I mean, you gotta give the guy credit for *trying,* you know. On his *own.* Without his wingman."

"Chuck is not looking for a soul mate, Hattie. He's looking for a body to warm his bed, nothing else."

Hattie sighed in exasperation.

"People change, you know." Her voice was strangely soft to Calliope's ears.

Calliope tensed, for she knew what her friend was going to say, and she could not stop her. But that did not mean Calliope wanted to hear it.

"All I'm saying, is you can't be a hermit forever, Callie. What happened with David—"

"Hattie, please..." She groaned. "Don't..."

Just the mention of the man who'd gotten into her heart... who'd held it in his hands and crushed her dreams along with it... it was enough to make Calliope scream.

Like so many of the men she'd encountered in her long life, she'd thought she was providing David Green a sound service—inspiring him to be the great writer he was meant to be. He was charismatic, bright, and his talent was severely malnourished and she knew with the right hand to guide him he could be an absolute star.

And when she'd offered him the same deal that she offered all her patrons, their dreams on a silver platter in exchange for the love and devotion she craved, she rationed David Green was worth it. His words, his art... it was all too important to *not* oversee.

And at first, the bond of praise and submission, the give and take, was heavily weighted. Calliope gave and gave all she could to feed into David's lofty ideals and dreams of grandeur. She had given him everything she could, including herself. Her heart. Her body. Until she had nothing left, no sparks left to give.

And he'd taken it all in greedily, spitting it back out in the form of a book—a book about Life and Death, as an entangled star-crossed lovers' tale.

It was a lovely tale of fiction, but he would never see its success. Not now, not ever again...

Calliope could feel the tears festering

behind her eyes. She did not want to think about David and his NYT bestselling book, *A Tangled Web*, which was apparently being made into a movie. She did not want to think about his dark laugh, or his nights of madness, hunched over his computer. And she certainly didn't want to think about his poetic, gifted words born from her spark and his madness, or the fact she'd been too late to save him.

It seemed, in the end, his darkness, his void—had too strong of a hold on the man, and no amount of inspiration could have enforced a will for him to *live*.

It had been nearly six months since he'd taken his own life, since Calliope felt the void form in her heart. And though she wanted more than anything to paint, to process the grief and pain, the guilt, she could not find it within herself to do so, and that fact, above all else, spoke to the depth of which David had altered the muse's very being.

She had loved him the same as she had those before him, but his words, his promises, were far too tempting to believe. He was a devil with his words, more so than Plato or Lord Byron or Poe. And so, Calliope fell down into David Green's dark void, making the gravest mistake of all.

She believed that he loved *her.* That he was her soul's *mate.*

But David Green was a wolf in sheep's clothing. He did not love anyone. He did not even love himself.

And Calliope could not find it within herself to take a patron or inspire anyone, since. And when the painting stopped, when the writing stopped, Calliope told herself it would pass. Every artist experienced a block in one way or another, and it always passed...

"I know that," she said carefully. "But you can not blame me for being cautious with my gifts when my gifts are a curse, clearly."

"Callie..."

Calliope drained the rest of her drink as the lights turned down low, the room shifting to a darkened ambience with the sudden influx of light illuminating candles all throughout the room.

"All right, my darlings, take your places!" Aphrodite called out. "Our Masquerade of Mystery starts in just five minutes!"

"Good luck, Hattie." Calliope shoved the empty martini glass across the bar and slid off her stool, relishing in the faint dizziness as her feet touched the ground. She blinked a few times, trying to filter in the sight of everything amidst the swaths of neon and candlelight. The room was full of life as everyone took their places and Calliope's heart pounded in her chest with anxiety and trepidation, and something else. Something she did not want to pay as much attention to for fear it would be damaging to her as well as her passions in life.

And just as Eve rang the bell and called out the start of the evening, Calliope felt the strangest force around her; like a vibration, an echo. It was warm and solid, and it felt somehow strange and familiar all at once. She opened her eyes as the buzzer sounded, laying her gaze on the man across from her, dressed in what looked like a blue button-down with the sleeves rolled up to his elbows and a black, plastic mask that reminded her of *Zorro*.

But it wasn't the sharp-dressed attire or the stocky build of the man that intrigued her. It was his eyes. Deep like phthalo green, bleeding into canvas, staining every untouched surface.

Calliope had never seen such eyes before and she couldn't help but think the darkness, the shadows of mystery surrounding them, added to the man's allure.

"So, do you like Piña Coladas?" he asked, his voice oddly awkward but with an overstated cockiness that mimicked humor, which told her he was not as confident on the inside as he was attempting to appear on the outside.

Interesting.

"That depends. Do you plan on buying me a Piña Colada, Zorro?" she coyly responded.

The man chuckled, his lips turning up into the corner into a sly grin. "Maybe."

She shook her head. "What ever happened to getting to know a woman first before you buy her a drink?"

"I mean... you can tell a lot about a woman by the type of drink she orders," he said, crossing his arms. His performative cockiness irritated her, but she also found it strangely refreshing. Because they were all here, pretending to be someone else, were they not? Hiding behind ornate masks and alluring costumes, hoping to feed into some sort of fantasy?

"I doubt that." She scoffed.

The man in front of her licked his lips, nodding to the table beside them where Hattie and a lithe man with a slender, gold venetian mask sat. Zorro nodded to Hattie's drink.

"Pomegranate martini. Equal parts bitter and sweet, which tells me *she* has two sides, and one of them is a side you don't want to be on. Red is usually symbolic of love and sex, which makes it a pretty bold statement in a place like this."

Calliope smirked. "And power. Fortune, too."

"Huh?"

"You said red is symbolic of love and sex, but anyone with a smartphone can Google that." She tutted. His mouth fell open and she let out a chuckle.

"You're lying," he said, with a scoff.

"I'm not. Red is also a symbol of victory and rebellion. And depending on the shade, it can also be toxic." She licked her lips proudly.

"It's also a color that symbolizes desire. Heat. Anger. Aggression." He shifted in his seat, but his smirk was enticing. His eyes lit up with excitement. He was enjoying this banter, this flirtation. And Calliope couldn't say she disliked it, either.

"That it is." She shifted in her seat, the motion making some dark hair spill out of her updo messily. "And what about you, Zorro? What do you prefer?"

The intriguing man shrugged. "Piña Coladas are my favorite. Especially the ones when they put those little cherries on top..." He puckered his lips, pretending to give a bon appétit gesture, as if the little candy cherries were truly a delicacy.

Callie shook her head but couldn't help the smile forming on her lips. "And what does your drink choice say about *you*?"

He leaned closer, across the table, his green eyes flashing up at her. "I like sweet things," he whispered.

"Is that so?"

He nodded, licking his lips. "Life's too short to be bitter, right?"

Calliope's gaze drifted to his pouty lips, parted just so. She was acutely aware of how close he was, close enough she could have easily closed the gap between them. The scent of his earthy cologne hit her like a stone, but it wasn't a terrible smell. In fact, she sucked in a small breath, letting the spicy notes fill her lungs as she met his verdant gaze.

Just as she considered the thought of speaking, of leaning in to respond, the startling buzzer sounded, nearly making her jump. Zorro pulled back, and the spell between them had been broken. It was time to move.

Already?

Calliope did not want Zorro to move.

But regardless of her wants, he stood carefully, sliding his hands in his pockets as he sauntered past her, capturing her gaze as he leaned into her space, whispering in her ear, "Was nice to meet you, Princess."

"Where are you going?" she breathed, acutely aware of the man taking a seat across from her.

Zorro smirked at her once more. His green eyes lit up behind his mask, full of mischief. "To get something sweet," he murmured.

And just as Zorro disappeared into the crowd, the buzzer sounded, pulling Calliope back to her present date as the room fell into chaos once more.

CHAPTER TWO

STAY COOL, STAY cool, don't look back.
Theo told himself as he headed toward the bar, his body shaking.

He wasn't sure what he expected to happen by going to the DeLux Cafe, despite the fact that he'd heard a lot of great things about it. Some of the guys in Theo's dorm were frequent flyers themselves—including his roommate, Patrick—aka Trick—and they all attended the speed date nights on account that they'd heard there were supernaturals that went there looking for human mates.

I'm not sure I believe in all that magic-fate stuff, even in my own realm. It's probably just a marketing ploy, but whatever the case, the guys are always raving about how hot the women are and how the drinks are some of the best in the city, so why not at least see what all the buzz is about, right? Theo surmised as much when Trick shoved a plastic mask at him and told him to put his big boy pants on because he was going with them tonight to this *Mystery Masquerade* thing at the DeLux Cafe, and he wasn't taking no for an answer.

"*You need* to get laid, *Theo.*" Trick said the words like Theo was going to die tomorrow if he didn't somehow find some beautiful woman to sink his cock into.

As if being a perpetually single twenty-four year ex-fiancé slash student who doesn't have time for a relationship between school, the gym, and now this new work study I'll be starting Monday, is a bad thing.

Theo's load wasn't huge this semester, with just fifteen credits, but since he'd put off all his electives the last couple of semesters, his schedule had become less stuff he *wanted to* do, and more requirements to graduate.

Seriously, what does a kinesiology major need Creative Writing and Painting 101 for? Though there was one particular class, Theo found himself interested in this semester—Lifestyle Drawing. Learning how to capture the body and movement from a different angle seemed like it might actually be helpful for him, even applicable, to some measure.

I'd be lying if I said I wasn't a little bit intrigued at the idea of drawing naked models for a couple hours out of the week. Theo wasn't an artist by any means, but sometimes he'd sketch doodles on his notes when he was bored.

Theo garnered that perhaps it might not be such a bad idea for him to zone out with his headphones and paint or doodle for a few hours, maybe even take a break from everything. But he was not going to tell Trick or the guys, that. Especially not when they were more interested in pre-gaming and snapping each other's masks like idiots.

Trick is right, though. I do need to put

myself out there. I don't want to be alone, it's just... easier, sometimes.

Theo's mind wandered even now to his friend's incessant nagging that Theo "get laid", while also worrying that perhaps his friend was too optimistic.

"The best way to get over someone, is to get underneath someone else, Theo," Trick had said, his voice tinged with sympathy. Though Theo didn't want to think about his failed relationships, or his lack of confidence when it came to women. Something Trick had taken upon himself to try and *fix*. As if enough pick up lines and parties would erase everything. Trick did not understand that Theo wanted *more*. And four years ago, he thought he'd had it when Emily said *yes* to his proposal at prom. But as he and his fiancé neared their prospective futures, yes turned to *no*. And when Theo had arrived at Emily's dorm, after a long two-year engagement, with flowers to surprise her on her birthday nearly three weeks into the semester only to find her with some jock, his pants around his ankles and his cock buried inside her, he knew the love he thought existed between him and his fiancé was a lie.

So Theo did the only thing he could. He broke off his engagement and focused on his studies, on himself. It was easier than allowing anyone into his heart again, for fear it would be demolished. But he was not impervious to loneliness. He missed being *with someone*. He missed late night summer makeouts and cuddling on the couch. He missed the spontaneity of discovering new things, and he certainly missed sex. But Theo garnered it was better this way. Happily Ever After, fate... all of it was a lie.

But Trick was not easily dismissed by Theo's admissions of a botched forever.

"You've got all the time in the world to get married, Theo. You're only young once, dude." Trick said after Theo had confessed his shattered engagement. Trick didn't understand. That was what Theo wanted more than anything else in the world.

He wanted Happily Ever After, a love that was forever. A woman he could cherish and love and give his whole heart—and his body—to.

How wrong he'd been. And even after their dissolved engagement, he had *tried* to move on. He'd even had sex once or twice, mostly because he felt like it was what his *dates* expected, and he rationalized perhaps it would help him out of his rut, but that only left him feeling empty and like shit, which was why he'd stopped and shifted his focus. Nothing felt quite right, and Theo was worried it never would.

But Trick wasn't about to let that be an excuse.

"I will get you laid, Theo, if it is the last thing I fucking do," Trick had said, before loading him into the Uber alongside him and his teammate, Shaun.

"I'm not like you, Trick. I don't have *game*. I'm awkward at best when it comes to flirting, and—"

"Fuck that self-deprecating bullshit, man. You have more to offer than you think, Theodore. Just think of it as practice tonight. A chance to put all you've learned from *me* to the test," Trick said as the car took off.

Theo sighed, knowing there was no use in arguing with the man. When Trick got something in his head, it was hard to convince the wide receiver to change his mind.

Theo looked out the window, watching as the lights blurred in the darkness.

"And if all else fails, man, at least there's the drinks!" Shaun said, his eyes like saucers.

Trick high-fived him before grabbing Theo's shoulder. "Amen to that."

Theo forced a smile, but it was not genuine.

Maybe Shaun's right, too. Maybe I just need to have a drink or two and relax. I can do that, right? Tonight doesn't have to be about getting laid. It can just be about talking to people, hanging out, sipping on some Piña Coladas.

Though even as Theo thought these things, he felt like a fish out of water. He was ashamed to admit how long it had been since he actually slept with someone at this point, or gone on a date that didn't end with a girl ghosting him. That was what Trick and his friends failed to understand. Theo *had* tried. To flirt, to date. Four years was a long time to be single. Especially when Trick and his friends were constantly having sex. Very loud, sometimes suspicious sex, in his dorm room.

Upon his descent from the Uber into the den of seduction that was the *Mystery Masquerade* at the DeLux Cafe,

Theo found himself on the edge of a precipice. Trick grabbed his shoulder, squeezing it with excitement and Theo rallied himself to do as Trick suggested.

Which was much easier after the two Piña Coladas he'd consumed so quickly, his nerves getting the better of him as he waited patiently for the event to start.

His goal was simple—it was just conversation, after all. Surely he was capable of conversing with a woman, and covering his face would likely provide an extra air of anonymity for Theo to hide behind.

Here, tonight, at the DeLux Cafe, Theo could pretend to be someone else.

Someone confident and cocky who knew how to flirt and please a woman, should the circumstances present itself.

He could pretend to be the man he

wanted to be. A man a woman would *want.* To keep.

Not some rejected perpetually single nerdy college student.

And just as the second fruity little drink hit him, the night began. He'd found his seat across from a lithe, beautiful woman wearing an ivory toga that clung to her curves deliciously. The tight pull of the fabric around her breasts enhanced her ample cleavage, elevating her pale skin. Her mask was a deep bronze, intricate, and looked far cooler than the black plastic mask Trick had likely picked up from *Party City.* But it wasn't her breasts or her lusciously dark, curled hair with its mysterious slivers of pink shining through that spilled out of her stylish updo that drew Theo to the woman before him. No, it was something else, some force he could not quite explain save for the fact it felt magnetic.

He could have sat anywhere in the cafe, but he'd chosen to sit there. It was almost as if fate had lured him there.

Theo did not believe in fate, but what if fate believed in him?

He didn't know her name. Nor did he know how old she was. Theodore Lange did not know anything, really, except that the minute he caught her amber gaze, he felt like she could see right through him. Underneath his mask, to his bloody soul. And that was as exhilarating as it was terrifying.

He'd never felt this way about anyone before, not even his ex-fiancé.

So, he did exactly as he had promised himself to do. He put Trick's teachings to the test. It was a miracle he'd remembered his ice breaker—a cheeky little bit about what a person's drink says about them, something he'd discerned from many nights out with Trick and his teammates—and he'd delivered the conversation without managing to look like an absolute fool.

And Miss Perfect—because as far as Theo was concerned, the goddess in front of him was the embodiment of perfection itself—had done the one thing Theo feared from the get-go.

She challenged his claim.

But Theo did not feel called out or on the spot by her rebuttal, nor did he feel angry that she had corrected him, and continued the conversation by educating *him*. No, Theo felt electrified and found his responses came easy, the banter between him and Miss Perfect sparking a desire within him he hadn't felt in years.

He was *flirting,* and successfully. And, it seemed, she was flirting with him as well, reciprocating and teasing him. Theo wanted *more.* He did not wish to entertain anyone else in the cafe. He only wanted more of the spark Miss Perfect had ignited within him.

Though, to be fair, it wasn't *all* Miss Perfect's charms that had Theo feeling alive and excited. Usually, it took a lot more than a couple fruity drinks to get Theo drunk, but Theo, like his friends, had been used to cheap beer and bottom shelf liquor. He was not prepared for the strength of his sweet frozen cocktails.

Or maybe it's just a change of scenery, a break, I don't fucking know. Whatever it is, I'm not fighting it. I feel relaxed and I'm having fun, Theo thought to himself as he stood tall and proud. His verdant gaze drifted to Miss Perfect, to her vibrant red lips, her eyelashes behind her mask fluttering as she looked up at him.

With a smile on her face.

Trick would be proud.

Come to think of it, where is Trick...

Theo scanned the room momentarily, looking for his friend, breathing a little easier when he saw him at a table in the corner talking to a woman, smiling his patented perfect football player smile.

Theo sucked in a breath as he coolly sauntered past Miss Perfect, hoping that his flirtations and insinuations, along with his offer to buy her a drink, would give him the result he truly wished for.

He knew it was a long shot; after all,

he'd only spoken with *one* woman and this was an hour-long speed dating event. She could have anyone in the room if she wanted them. He knew that. It was foolish to think she'd *want him,* when there were certainly many more men to choose from; men who came prepared to this event and probably had much more to offer her in terms of conversation and attraction. But something inside him told him he'd made the right move. No one else in this cafe would make him feel quite as bold and confident, make him feel as if he *could* take a shot like this. Miss Perfect was clearly out of his league. But as confident as Theo felt at the moment, his conscience threatened to poison his fantasy moment with a dose of reality.

If you had her interest, she wouldn't

be at that table right now. She'd be following you. The voice in his head bit, trying to squash his sudden burst of confidence.

Which is why I have to focus on walking as calmly as I can to the bar and not turning around once more to look and see if Miss Perfect Princess is looking at that other guy at the table instead of me, he thought, sliding his heated hands in his dark pants pocket. The red lights strewn about cast an eerie glow over the bar itself, and the heavy bass beats got louder as he pushed past the mingling singles toward the bar to find an available stool.

It seemed most of the men and women were not as quick to cash in their chips as he was, and for that reason, alone, he relished the emptiness of the bar and the speed of the drink delivery.

Maybe I showed my cards too early. Maybe I should have been a little more mysterious or whatever, but fuck, I don't want to waste another second entertaining anyone else when she leaves me feeling like this.

"What can I get ya?" the bartender asked nonchalantly.

"I'll have another Piña Colada, please." He took his seat.

The white-haired woman nodded and went about her business, pouring the icy liquid into glass, and garnishing it with an abundance of fruit and a cherry before sliding it to him.

The inkling to turn around and see if Miss Perfect was still there, sitting in her seat, staring at some other man, was prevalent, but Theo told himself if fate was truly on his side, she would find her way to him. And Theo had decided, speed date or not, he was going to stay at that bar all night if that was what it took.

"What about you, sweetheart?" the bartender's voice pulled Theo from his thoughts, and the familiar scent of vanilla and spice assaulted his senses, causing him to spin to his side to see who the bartender was speaking to. He nearly jumped out of his chair when he saw *her*. Miss Perfect. His *Princess*.

Her long, slender arms reached out to brace her hands on the edge of the bar, tendrils of her dark hair tucked behind her ears, framing her mask. She'd been breathtaking before, when all he could see was half of her. *A very hot half, I might add.*

But standing before him, Theo could take in the entirety of this goddess's beauty.

Her long, slender pale legs jutting out from the slits in her toga sparkled in the low light, and the motion as she propped her leg out drew attention to the sinful curve of her back, her tight, round ass standing out. Her form was exquisite, but it wasn't her breasts or her ass or even her slender fingernails that pulled his attention.

It was her eyes; amber irises hidden behind a dark mask that called to him. That enticed him. He got the feeling that if he let himself, he could get lost in her amber gaze.

"I'll have a Piña Colada, extra pineapple, please," she said sweetly, her voice soft like a bell.

Theo couldn't help the smile that formed on his face. "Was starting to think you'd lost your appetite," he said, before sucking down a fresh, icy bout of his frozen drink through his straw. Unfortunately, he'd been too overzealous and the instant brain freeze caused him to seize up, scrunching his shoulders and squinting his eyes as he hissed, the frozen bits oozing out the top of his straw.

"Fuck," he bit as he closed his eyes.

Miss Perfect giggled, but the sound was as charming as a wind chime.

"Open your eyes," Miss Perfect casually commanded, and Theo tensed, trying to combat the cool air spreading through him that was making him shiver.

He did not hesitate to do as she asked, without thinking, noting the way she was staring at him through her mask, her eyes glowing almost golden in the light.

It's a trick of this lighting, for sure. People's eyes don't glow like that. His gaze settled on hers, his conscience once again trying to explain the strange thoughts and feelings coursing through him.

He'd only just met the woman, but she felt strangely familiar. As if he'd seen her somewhere before, but he couldn't quite place her. But such things were hard to discern with half her face hidden.

Miss Perfect reached out for him, her fingertips moving some stray golden-brown hair out of his eyes, off his forehead. Her nails tickled his skin, but she didn't drop her hand. Instead, she just massaged his temples, and Theo started to feel a little warmer all over. And a little less tense.

"I nearly did. Lose my appetite," she said smoothly, her fingertips gently grazing his skin as she touched his cheek.

Theo could not move, nor could he take his eyes off of her. He tried to think of a name, a color that would describe the depth and warmth, but nothing fit. Not gold or ochre or amber felt pristine and rich enough.

I don't know the shade, or the name, but fuck. They are beautiful. She's beautiful. Even behind a mask.

"Oh, really?" Theo asked, shifting closer to her with his own seat.

Miss Perfect dropped her fingers from his face, her gaze dipping to his lips before she took her own drink in her hand, delicately and demurely sipping her liquid through the straw.

"Mhmm." she murmured, licking her lips when she was done.

No brain freeze for Miss Perfect, obviously. God, I'm so out of my fucking league, clearly.

"What changed your mind?" Theo asked, without thinking. His voice sounded darker to his own ears than he knew it should. He returned to his drink, this time slowly sucking some liquid through his straw, careful not to overdo it again.

Though if overdoing it means she gets to touch my face and make my skin all tingly again, I'll take it...

Miss Perfect batted her eyelashes at him, giving Theo a sweet, yet seductive grin.

"Sometimes, you just get a craving for something and you can't stop thinking about it." Her gaze drifted to the rim of his drink, hovering for a moment over his untouched fruit before her attention was back on her own drink.

"I feeling the know," Theo said stupidly, because apparently his damn brain freeze had made him forget how to speak properly. "I mean, I know the feeling," he said, letting out a chuckle as he tried to recover from his momentary blunder. "But I can't say I don't like it. The... feeling. Craving something sweet, I mean." Theo felt as if he was grasping at his sanity, and it wasn't because of the alcohol.

No, not entirely, anyway. For as he fought his blush, as he gazed upon Miss Perfect and her amber eyes, the reality dawned on him she had taken him up on his offer. She was *interested.* Otherwise, why would Miss Perfect have come to the bar to share a drink with him if she was not intrigued by him and his sudden burst of confidence?

And that reality—that understanding that perhaps she felt the same attraction—was equally as terrifying as it was exciting.

The night, as it seemed, was going rather smoothly for him. It was turning out to be the best night ever for one Theodore Lange.

But certainly he'd screw it up somehow, right?

He let out a heavy breath, trying to

push his vicious anxieties aside.

No, think positive thoughts, Theo! Don't fuck this up!

At some point, the polite conversation and fantastical flirtations would cease, and the question would need to be asked if perhaps they should take their newfound attractions elsewhere. Theo had never done such a thing before. Taken a woman *home* from a bar.

He didn't make it a habit of visiting bars and hitting on beautiful women like Trick or his friends. Aside from the two times he'd met up with people off of the dating apps he'd tried, which were not the best experiences, and his one serious relationship that ended abruptly and left him blindsided—Theo wasn't sure how one approached such a topic. Was it presumptuous to ask now?

Should he wait? What if she said no?

Oh God, what if she says yes?

The panic started to fester in his brain, and he nearly choked on his drink at the thought.

If he was lucky enough to get that far with Miss Perfect, he rationalized he would think about it then. Perhaps that was a problem for future Theodore. Present Theodore needed to focus so he would not end up with a brain freeze or start choking on his drink again like an imbecile if he did indeed wish to make it out of the cafe with Miss Perfect.

He watched as she plucked a cherry from atop her glass. Its bright red maraschino skin caught the neon red light, making it almost glow like hard candy.

He licked his lips, and she smiled at

him.

"See something you like, Zorro?"

He shrugged affably as he smirked, letting out a chuckle of his own. "I don't know who the fuck this Zorro is that you keep speaking of, but the answer is yes." He bit his lip. "I think I do. See something I like. Very much." Perhaps he was too emboldened as he mused over how forward he was being, but when Miss Perfect's cheeks pinked at his words and she shook her head, smiling back at him so carefree, he felt more than validated. Her coy smile was cuter than it should have been, the faint pink tones beneath her mask contrasting her pale skin and turning shades of magenta from the lights. The sight made Theo feel strangely warm all over. His skin was practically buzzing.

Theo watched as she gracefully extended the little ball of fruit, holding it out gingerly in the space between them. Her amber gaze beckoned him like a siren to the sea. Tempting him, luring him. His gaze narrowed on the bright red cherry and he got the feeling that what Miss Perfect was offering him was so much more than fruit. But that'd be crazy, right?

I mean, this is a speed dating party. It's not like I'm actually going to find my soulmate here or anything. It's just... practice. A test.

A chance to prove that I'm not a lost cause.

"Not a fan of cherries?" he asked, his voice tinged with gravel from his drink and the charged tension as the cherry dangled between them like a lifeline.

"I'm not sure this actually qualifies as fruit," she said with a giggle. "I prefer the real thing. But you did say you liked *sweet things*."

Theo smirked before leaning forward to bite the cherry out of her hand, stem and all, pulling it into his mouth in one fell swoop.

Miss Perfect let out a soft gasp, clearly not expecting the brush of his lips on her knuckles as he stole his fake fruit prize.

His teeth worked the pliable bulb off the stem, relishing the sweet candy taste in his mouth, swallowing the fruit while keeping the stem in his mouth, if only to tie it into a knot for no other reason than he thought it would look cool. Trick and the boys didn't care for his cherry knot tying skills, and therefore, he'd never been able to illustrate the bar trick for a woman before.

Miss Perfect didn't seem to mind, though, as Theo noticed her gaze drift to his mouth, pulling her own lower lip between her teeth, and he felt strangely warm and aroused by her barely inaudible gasp.

His cock stiffened in his pants and he shifted his position to not draw too much attention. He did not wish to put the cart before the horse, and he wasn't sure how one might perceive such a reaction in a public setting.

The instant thought of her discovering his sudden erection in a room full of people should have been like a bucket of cold water to his system, but it was the opposite. He shifted once more, trying to keep his wits about him as moisture pebbled at his cockhead, pressing against the inside of his briefs. It took much more concentration than it should have for him to ignore his twitching cock and focus on his tongue.

When he was done, he spat the stem out and set it on the red napkin on the bar, next to his drink, before catching Miss Perfect's attention again.

"Tastes pretty good to me." He flashed her a grin, feeling bolder than ever. Something about this woman made him feel as though he was truly the only man in the room. He felt braver in her presence.

She shook her head, sipping her drink once more before flashing her gaze back at Theo, her sights landing on the rim of his half-drunk glass, right over his pineapple.

Theo carefully plucked the wedge from the rim, holding it out to her in the space she held the cherry. "You did say you wanted extra pineapple," he said with a grin.

Miss Perfect looked at the fruit between his fingers, and he did not miss the way she sucked in a breath. For she looked at that slice of fruit as if she was *starving.* Theo's stomach flipped, his blood rushing beneath the surface. No woman had ever looked at *him* the way Miss Perfect was eyeing up his tropical offering.

Oh to be a fucking pineapple...

She reached her fingers out carefully, almost hesitantly.

"I promise it's not poisoned," he said, trying to make light of the strange tension between them.

"I wouldn't think so," she said, her voice dark and smooth, like decadent fudge.

Theo *loved* fudge.

"For the record, all you have to do is ask," he said, the sticky sweet acid staining the edge of his thumb. "If you want me." All at once, he'd realized his error, and just like that, the real Theo shone through his cocky Trick-inspired facade. Heat rushed into his cheeks. But instead of feeling bad about his blunder, he found the slip of his tongue a relief.

The truth was much simpler than the lie, was it not?

Theo implored her gaze, feeling as if a weight had been lifted from his shoulders. Miss Perfect did not scoff or roll her eyes at his Freudian slip. In fact, she gazed back at him, her lips tugging up into a small smile that was somehow as endearing as it was seductive as a light giggle escaped her throat.

"It. If you want *it*, I mean, the fruit. All you need to do is say 'please, Zorro,' and I'll give it to you." His taunt seemed to get another sweet giggle out of her and the sight made him smile. Not because her ruby red lips and perfect smile were like something out of a movie, but because it was *his* doing. He'd made her *laugh*.

More than once. And that itself was a victory for Theodore Lange.

He felt as if he'd just discovered some uncharted territory, and perhaps he had. But he was also quite certain, all mishaps aside, that the fantastic Piña Coladas had definitely gone to his head, and in conjunction with his fiery victory, he decided to take the plunge, blurting out, "I'll give you anything you want."

Miss Perfect bit her lip, letting out a contented sigh as she reached for the fruit, causing Theo's blood to rush again. He was starting to sweat.

I think I need some air...

The room around Theo started to spin, the air getting thinner as his heartbeat quickened. It was as if time was somehow slowing down, but speeding up all at once.

Her fingers grazed his as she slowly plucked the fruit from his hands. "Is that so?" she whispered.

Theo nodded, suddenly at a loss for words. "Uh huh."

There was a strange truth to his words. There were a multitude of things he didn't know about Miss Perfect. He didn't know her name, her favorite color, what she did for a living, if she was a student like him, or if she had graduated and gone on to better opportunities, and he certainly didn't know what it was she wanted in a man, nor did he have any idea if he even *met* a fraction of her requirements. And in truth, she did not know him, either.

But what Theo *did* know, for absolute certainty, was that he meant those words with the utmost sincerity. He would give Miss Perfect *anything* she wanted, if only she asked.

Simply because he *wanted* to. He had so much *to* give if only the right person would give him the chance.

Could Miss Perfect be that person?

He watched as she slid the wedge of fruit into her mouth, sucking the juice out before biting down hard, the sight causing his cock to twitch once more in his dress pants, suddenly acutely aware of how hot he was. Heat ransacked his body like a fire.

Is the air conditioning on in this place? Or have we descended into hell?

Theo slurped his drink, noting the glass itself was starting to sweat as if it, too, could not handle the heat that being in this woman's presence seemed to spark.

Miss Perfect swallowed her bite of fruit just as a sliver of juice trickled down her chin. Theodore did not think, he only reacted on impulse. He reached out, wiping the juice up with his thumb, immediately sticking his finger in his mouth afterward. He could taste the sweetness of the pineapple mixed with the faint taste of *her*. Or more aptly, her sweat, since it was damn hot in the room.

Some dark hair spilled out of her messy updo, falling over her shoulder, and the heavy scent of vanilla and spice filled his lungs.

Her gaze *glowed*, for the faintest moment. Like a golden moon in the night sky, like a shimmer of glitter in the darkness.

"Anything?" she whispered, leaning into his space. Her crimson-stained lips ghosted over his as if she was afraid, but of what, Theo had no clue.

What could she be afraid of? What does a woman like Miss Perfect have to fear?

But something about that vulnerability, Miss Perfect's faint hesitation, called to him. He wanted to hear her say the words, but he got the feeling the permission she needed was *his* permission. His assurance. And that resonated with Theo deeper than anything else. For he knew what it was to want, to crave. To want to take a leap of faith and plunge headfirst.

As Theo gazed up at the object of his current fixation from beneath his mask, he held her gaze steady. He'd never felt so powerful in his life.

"Anything, Princess," he whispered as he closed the remaining distance between them and crushed his mouth against hers.

CHAPTER THREE

ZORRO'S LIPS MOVED slowly against hers, carefully at first. His kiss was almost hesitant, but bold at the same time. Like he was unsure of such a forward move, perhaps even unsure if she would respond, but he'd taken the shot anyway because he couldn't bear *not* to know. And as his lips curiously danced along hers, she could not help but respond in unison.

Calliope had kissed many men—and

even some women—and plenty of her patrons had written about, sang about, or illustrated sentiments about the perfect kiss. But Calliope had never felt a perfect kiss before. Not until this moment as her masked prince's warm, smooth lips settled everything around her.

And so she did not fight the fire inside of her that threatened to burn, to consume, either. It'd been too long since Calliope had felt such a spark.

The softest sound escaped his throat as his tongue slid into her mouth without hesitation, the strokes slow and deliberate, reverent almost.

With every caress of his tongue and soft motion of his silken lips, Calliope felt herself slipping. The lines between want and need felt as if they were being stretched taut, and the lines were going to snap. She knew she was playing with fire, but Calliope *missed* fire. She missed its warmth, its intensity. She missed dancing in the flames. For such was the life of a muse—always sparking, always igniting someone's passion—until, of course, the fire burned down to embers, unable to sustain its heat any longer. Or died, altogether.

Calliope's shoulders loosened and she felt the faintest heat on her neck, her flesh. In her blood. Her charming Zorro settled his hand against her throbbing vein, his palm hot, the touch smooth. She could not help but feel overwhelmed by him. By his kiss, his touch, his earthy, spicy cologne. For the moment, there was pure bliss. There was only them, in this moment, existing inside time itself as well as outside of it. Her insides heated like a fire and that familiar jolt, that *spark* she'd longed to feel again, returned with renewed vigor, rising from the ashes like a phoenix as the air thinned around her.

Who is this man? Where has he been hiding?

The mysterious masked stranger continued his torturously slow, seductive kiss, gently sucking her bottom lip before grazing his tongue over it. The act, however small it was, was full of untapped desire. A deep sound escaped him, something akin to a deep whispered moan, like a desperate prayer. In that one swift motion, that faint caress of his tongue as he kissed her bottom lip, she could feel *everything* bubbling beneath the surface.

Everything this perfect man kept buried. His determination, his passion, his drive.

And all at once, the spark flourished, the rush of flames catching on the brittle remnants of the dried leaves and wood Calliope had strewn over her broken, coffined heart.

Flashes of color flooded her vision. Bursts of bright, victorious red, fading into deep, dark shades of green, like a forest on fire. She settled her hand on his neck, feeling his racing pulse beneath her fingertips.

Did he feel it, too? This spark? This undeniable *fire*?

Did he understand what power those words held for her?

Anything you want. Anything, Princess.

Calliope had never truly seen herself

as a figure of royalty, and though many men had called her Princess—or kitten or baby, and even sweetheart—there was an offering in the way her perfect stranger spoke such devotion.

Oh, Zorro... you do not understand the words you speak.

Calliope knew he did not understand. How could he? For starters, he was drunk—as was she—but he was also a human. And humans rarely understood the depth of their words and promises, Calliope had learned.

He's no different than the other men I've entertained, Calliope thought, trying to combat the ease of which she felt to fall into this man and give him everything he desired.

Whatever that may be. She wasn't sure what he truly desired because she could not see it in her mind's eye the way she usually could with the people she inspired. The spark *always* knew what a man or woman needed from her to thrive, and perhaps if Calliope had not been so lost in the perfection of his kiss and the sweet taste of pineapple on his tongue along with the haze of the alcohol she'd consumed, she may have realized how important that little fact was.

Because a muse's purpose was to inspire those who would change the world—with the help of her patronage, of course.

But there was only one person who could truly inspire a muse, one person who could change their immortal fate, and they would be blind to their deepest desire, because their truest desire would be their *mate.*

Their divined mate, of course.

At the faintest thought of the myth that was a muse's mate, memories flashed through her brain of Chuck and of David. Of all the promises they'd made in vain. Chuck had called her his soulmate, on more than one occasion. David as well. But David also called her the devil, too. And oh, how blind she had been when it came to David and his *truest* desire.

"If only I could just feel the spark," he cried, angrily shoving the papers on the desk. The memory of him on his knees, eyes imploring her with tears pushed forth, trying to sour the perfect moment. It was a warning, a cautionary instinct.

Because Calliope knew just what could happen if she let herself forget. If she gave in too easily to the spark inside of her. She needed to protect it.

Because love—was not for muses. It was for the patrons, the men and women who desired her gifts, who *needed* her love to become the philosophers and artists and musicians that were meant to change the world.

Greatness could not be achieved without the power of a muse's praise, after all. The love she gave was never equal. It was never reciprocated. Chuck had proved that years ago, and Calliope surmised perhaps then, it was better to separate her own wants and needs from the work she had to do.

And for centuries, Calliope had accepted that fate. That no one would ever *love* her or desire her in the way she truly wanted.

She'd deluded herself into believing

David was different. His writings and musings were captivating, and the moments she allowed herself to feel love for him, were as shattering as they were beautiful. Because no matter how much Calliope gave, she never felt whole, she never felt the *spark.*

She fought the urge to slip down memory lane, not wanting to think of their heated tryst the night they'd met in the *Den of Sin,* or their whirlwind affair, of his cursed words that would forever haunt her. But it was no use. They were too similar to Zorro's breathless pleas.

"I'll do anything, Callie. Please, just give me a spark to get through these pages..."

That was what Calliope's patrons failed to understand. For every spark Calliope gave them, the more pain it caused her, the more it drained her. And when there was nothing left to give them, her job was done. And the inevitable downfall would rain on the muse and her patrons and leave her alone once more, dying to find the next man or woman to bring it back.

No one could ever sustain it, least of all Calliope. Because the universe had created her to be infinite, and a soulmate who could sustain her spark would take that away.

It was a cruel existence for a muse. To love and lose, over and over again, for the sake of humanity and its advancements.

But for the moment, Calliope was not loving or losing. She was living inside the electrified energy that existed between her and a stranger, in the most perfect kiss. She moved her mouth against his, shoving the poisonous thoughts away. His hand slid up her neck, into her hair, and he tightened his grip, holding her still. Calliope relished in the force of his grip as it grounded her. She kissed him with hunger, craving to hear those words once more.

Anything you want.

Oh, sweet devotion. Cruel, bloody devotion. It would be her undoing.

When her mysterious Zorro broke away from their heated, perfect kiss, her lips tingled, the energy between them still crackling in the air.

She gazed back at him, at his kiss-swollen, plump lips. At his jeweled gaze and dilated pupils. The energy between them was unlike anything she'd ever felt before, and it was far too tempting to resist.

But that was why she came to the DeLux tonight, was it not? She came to find a muse of her own, a spark to ignite the inspiration she'd lost. A person to make her forget about the pain of her loss, the pain of love.

Was Zorro that man? She wasn't sure.

But one thing she was sure of was that she'd never met or kissed anyone like him in her entire life, and that was enough for Calliope at the moment. Soon enough, the night would end, and reality would return. If all Calliope had was a moment to feel like *this* she wanted to live in the moment as long as she could.

"I think we should go," Calliope said, tasting the words on her tongue. They felt foreign, but also exhilarating.

CALLIOPE

This is probably a terrible idea. I'm not entirely sober, and Zorro isn't, either. This could end a total disaster. But something told her it was only just the beginning, and she'd had too much to drink to refute hope like that.

Zorro nodded, grabbing her hand and pulling her off her chair, toward the exit of the cafe. She let him pull her through the crowd, her hand in his palm heating like a fire. His fingers curled around hers and the spark, the energy between them, could be felt like it was an entity all its own.

"Your place or mine?" he asked, his voice breathless, yet somehow smooth and vulnerable. As if he were surprised at her boldness, but eager to continue stoking the obvious fire between them. Cars whizzed past them, but they were white noise to Calliope.

"My place," she responded without haste. With the way she was feeling, reeling from his kiss and the magnetic energy between them, she wanted to be close to her studio, in case the inspiration she'd been looking for caught. She knew it was wishful thinking, but part of her dared to hope. Something about this man, this Zorro, made her feel that spark of hope and desire she thought she'd long forgotten.

Anything you want, Princess.

The truth struck her almost as hard as his kiss.

"Calliope," she whispered.

"Huh?" Her charming stranger turned to look at her, his phthalo eyes catching the glimmer of the streetlights above them. Even under the lights with his kiss-swollen lips parted, hair blowing in the breeze, Calliope couldn't deny the man was a godly sight all on his own, even with the mask he wore.

Especially with the mask he wears...

"My name is Calliope," she repeated as she pulled out her phone from her slender purse clutch. Her fingers shook as she queued up a ride for the both of them, her heart racing as the reality of what she was doing hit her. But as she glanced up to look at her Zorro, she felt that undeniable energy pulsing like a sonar and the noise inside her quieted.

"But my friends call me Callie."

She could not deny the heat of his gaze as he watched her. It should have been creepy, or even bothersome, but Calliope did not feel such things. She only felt as if she wanted to remain under that dark, intense green gaze forever.

"Calliope," he murmured, tasting her name on his tongue. It was the most seductive sound, and then that flicker of seduction turned cheeky, sweet. "Like the chick from Hercules?"

Calliope couldn't help the faint giggle that escaped her throat at the naive sincerity in his voice. There was a youthfulness to his tone, which told her he was probably young. Old enough to drink, but not old enough to know a muse outside of the famous cartoon movie. Which should have bothered her more than it did, but then again, Calliope was, by mortal standards, also young. She was created, molded into the body of a timeless woman, her features and beauty adjusting along with the beauty standards of time itself. Physically, in this present time, she had morphed into the body of a woman in her late twenties, early thirties, which worked in her favor, both in her personal life and her professional life. Even in the supernatural realms, amongst the gods and goddesses, she was revered as an eternal beauty, a youthful spirit, even though she was not much younger than Hattie or Athena.

But she'd also spent so many years *being* young and effervescent, that she felt quite old. At least in comparison to most of the twenty-somethings that showed up at the university.

Which was another reason she'd felt so drawn to David, a man in his late forties desperate for more than his careful, curated life.

It was refreshing at first. He was older, wiser, and it was clear he had a message, something to say. She felt the ache in his throat, in his very being, when she touched him. But that ache was so much more than a desperate attempt to speak his truth. It was a dark void, kept at bay by his unattainable dreams. And when Calliope gifted him everything he wanted, the gates that held that void shattered.

And it grew. Poisoning everything and everyone in its path, including her.

Calliope stared back at the young Zorro, at his dilated pupils, his kiss-swollen lips. Even in the light of the streetlamps, she could see his clothes were fairly basic. A deep blue button down, the sleeves rolled up to his elbows, and a pair of black dress pants.

But it was his shoes—black and white Converses—that stood out as the most visible sign of his youth.

Though Calliope preferred many of the finer things in life, as was the desire of a muse, she could not help but appreciate the sight of this man, in all his glory. Young and sweet. Full of life. Of hope.

And perhaps that was what Calliope craved more than anything else. *Hope.*

She shook her head, dispelling her momentary stare, not wanting to be awkward. She captured his gaze with hers, her soul pleading with his to somehow understand what she could not say. Though she knew he couldn't.

Even if they were sober, under different circumstances, he wouldn't understand what she was offering.

Love me. Love me and I will give you everything you desire...

Everything you want.

Unfortunately, everything Calliope wanted was not something she could ever truly obtain. Because she was created to inspire humanity, with her voice, her words, her beauty. She was meant to be worshipped for her gifts and not her soul.

"Like the muse," she whispered, her heart wanting nothing more than to be known, to be seen in all her nakedness at that very moment. For him to know the truth. About her, about her curse. About what she wanted, truly.

But there on the street in the crisp LA night, she was not just a muse. She was just a woman who wanted to feel alive and inspired.

Offering her name to a stranger was dangerous all on its own. It made her vulnerable, it gave him power over her.

But Calliope was not thinking straight. The desire within her to connect, to feel that spark of hope and fire this stranger was able to somehow make her feel, was too tempting.

And it had been too long that she'd felt inspired and alive in the way this man made her feel. And if she was being honest, no man or woman had ever gotten to her so easily. So effortlessly.

Calliope knew the morning would come and wash away this perfect moment.

Because morning always came for a muse, and once Zorro had his fill of her magical charms, once he'd obtained that spark he desired, he'd go on his way.

Create something wonderful, perhaps even change the world.

But Calliope rationalized that she could handle it. She was no stranger to being left, and as long as she remembered her place, remembered to hold back her heart, she would be fine. He was a means to an end, a spark to ignite her long-dead and burned out fire. There were plenty before him, and perhaps he was only a stepping stone to the plenty after him. But in order to get there—back to her life as a muse, back to her canvas—she needed him, even if it was only for a night.

I want it all. I want everything this masked prince is willing to give me.

Even if it's just for a night.

One spark of inspiration is all I need...

It had been ages since Calliope had

taken a lover home.

To her private space. She'd learned early in her actual youth, it was much easier to be what her patrons needed, to serve them where they would be most inspired. And perhaps, she felt a sort of detachment in doing so that kept her protected. She needed a space she could work without distraction, a place to rest her heart as much as her head. A place untouched by heartbreak and desire. A temple of her own.

Home was always the one place Calliope could tire away and forget about her immortal muse curse. It was the one place where she could paint and write and exist without having to be someone for someone else. In the space of her apartment, she could be herself. Not Calliope the muse, but Calliope the *woman.*

David had only visited her off-campus apartment a few times, and those times had been troublesome, not desirable. He'd only come to Calliope's door begging for his spark, his inspiration in fits of madness because he couldn't write. He couldn't sleep. The voices in his head weren't *loud* enough.

Though Calliope felt they were louder than anything else.

Something about this realization made her tense, like an angel on her shoulder beckoning her to be careful. Letting a man into her personal space could be dangerous. She didn't *know* him. She did not even know his name. For all she knew, he could have been a serial killer who loved to prey on beautiful masked women.

Do not be silly, Calliope, you are a better judge of character than that.

While she knew enough to know her perfect stranger was probably not going to murder her, she still knew the danger was there. The mistakes were surmountable at this point, but Calliope did not care. The spark was too hungry. She was already in for a penny, why not go in for the whole pound?

Before she could process or hold onto her diminishing self-preservation, her masked Prince Charming's hands pulled her close, under the illuminating streetlights and his mouth found hers once more, and the world stopped.

Oh, sweet death, this man's kiss is a weapon all on its own.

"Calliope," he murmured drunkenly, with a deep rasp that made her insides twist. It was part whisper, part prayer. She could only imagine how it would sound in a temple, echoing off the walls. His voice dropped an octave.

"But you can call me *Callie*," she whispered.

He leaned into her space, running his nose up her neck as he breathed her in. The motion was strangely erotic, even though she knew it was just drunk impulse. Still, impulse or not, Calliope could not help but shiver from the sheer feel of his lips grazing her neck.

"Theodore," he muttered against my neck. "Like the chipmunk," he chuckled. "But you can call me Theo." His tone darkened once again, the rumble in his tenor making her blood rush. Calliope was acutely aware of the moisture blooming between her thighs as his smooth voice drowned the world out around her.

The image of *Theo*, on his knees, hands on his thighs while he stared at her with such *adoration*, mask and all, filled Calliope's psyche, and she let out an unavoidable groan.

"Theo..." she breathed his name, her lustful voice strange to her own ears after so long. It was like she was someone else, for the moment anyway.

Calliope wrapped her arms around him, her clutched phone dragging along his back as she tightened her grip on it in her hand while getting lost in his sweet, perfect kiss once more. She only let up when the sound of a blaring horn honked and the driver started yelling at them to get in.

Ah, that must be our ride.

The two of them parted for a moment, if only to catch their breaths. "Come, Theo," Calliope muttered, dragging Theo across the pavement. He stumbled a bit before letting go, if only to open the door for her to get in.

"After you, *Callie*," he said, the sound of her name on his tongue like music to her ears. Callie's grin brightened from the polite gesture, as it seemed men nowadays did not go out of their way to show their manners anymore and she could not deny this pleased her. But politeness was forgotten the moment they got into the car, the heat rising between them as Theo settled on the backseat next to her, shutting the door. Not a moment sooner was Calliope pulling Theo back to her lips, her fingers finding his neck once more. He did not fight her forwardness, and for that, she was rather grateful. Instead, he parted his lips, groaning in submission as she slid her tongue into his mouth. He tasted like sugar and coconut cream. Combined with his spicy, earthy scent, it was quite an intoxicating cocktail all on its own.

Calliope let herself slip once more, losing herself in the feel of his tongue in her mouth, his pulse beneath her palm. The spark inside her grew and the desire, the hunger inside of her grew with it.

The spark was always relentless, always seeking more, greedy like a spoiled child. *It's never enough. It will never be enough, because no one will ever worship* me. *For me.*

Humans were always drawn to a

muse, like moths to a flame. Whether they knew it or not, their bodies, their souls *craved* what Calliope and other muses could give them. They worshipped the gifts they received, not the muse themselves. Humans only desired their spark of inspiration, the magic that would change their lives forever.

A number one single.

A masterpiece of art.

A bestselling novel.

But no one had ever, truly worshipped *Calliope.* She thought David was different. Thought that he wanted her beneath all of the gifts and inspiration she had given him. She thought he'd do anything *for her.* But she was wrong.

I'm probably wrong about Theo, too. And perhaps that's truly my curse. I always know better, but desire is a demon that is too hard to fight.

So she did not fight it. Not one bit.

Calliope let Theo pull her into his lap in the back of the car, reveling in the momentary high as his mouth traveled along her neck, as his hands slid underneath her toga.

She let him slam her against her door, his mouth kissing every inch of her face, neck, and chest he could reach as they stumbled across her threshold, eliciting sighs of pleasure and wonder from her throat as his quick hands slid beneath the cool fabric of her costume and lifted her up. His hands settled beneath her thighs, grabbing her ass as he squeezed lightly, and she wrapped her legs around him. He held her tight, through his stumbling as he carried her into her apartment, her motion lights turning on and bathing them both in faint illumination.

With Theo's hands on her, everything felt right in a way it hadn't felt in a long time. He set her down, if only to adjust his evident hardness, and Calliope bit her lip as she took in the sight of him, here in her apartment like this. His dark hair falling over his mask, the faintest sheen of sweat on his neck. His dress pants pulling tight and the vivid outline of his cock. The spark inside her flourished into a flame as she felt the desire in her veins thrumming beneath the surface.

Calliope took one step forward, pushing Theo back against the arm of her couch as she made to unbutton his shirt, taking his mouth once more against her own. He parted his lips for her, giving her access to his tongue once more as she undressed him hastily. He shrugged off his shirt, her hands sliding over his hardened chest. But Theo made no move to grind himself against her or push her. Instead, his hands reverently worked at untying her sashes as she shimmied out of her toga until she was left in nothing but her strapless bra and panties. She slid her hands across his hips, pulling him and his hardness against her as they continued to kiss and touch one another, their hands moving of their own possessed accord.

Calliope unbuttoned his pants with rampant attention, and Theo stumbled beneath her as he all but hopped out of his pants, strewing them across the floor. Calliope felt emblazoned by the sight of this perfect man and she could not help the heat flushing her body or the excitement she felt under his sensual gaze. She settled her hands on his hips, pulling him, leading him like a lamb to the slaughter. And perhaps, in a way, he was nothing but a lamb. A naive, darling little creature, and she was quite the vicious wolf in the midst of her spark's desire.

Theo did not protest or hesitate as he followed her lead into her bedroom.

In the light of her studio apartment, her bedroom, his skin looked almost golden, his muscles standing out with perfect definition. Calliope's gaze traveled across his pecs, down to his chiseled hips and his perfect Adonis belt and his evident bulge in his tight, dark blue briefs. In combination with his mask, he looked like something out of her wildest dreams.

Oh Gods, is he perfect.

"Tell me what you want, Callie," he whispered as he took two steps toward her, backing her into the room. His voice was soft, hazy, but full of hope she could not refute. It was a rather intoxicating sound, those words on his tongue.

"I want to look at you," she whispered as she looked up at him from beneath her mask. She sucked in a breath, carefully grazing her fingers along the side of his mask.

"May I?" she asked, her voice barely a whisper, despite the fact no one else could hear them. But there was a vulnerability, a sort of tension in the air because she knew the moment she truly saw him, it would be over. There would be no way she could forget him.

And perhaps that was the most dangerous choice of all.

Theo nodded, swallowing harshly. "I told you," he murmured. "All you have to do is ask."

Calliope watched as he licked his lips and she gracefully settled her fingers on the sides of his mask. The cool plastic against her fingertips melded with the heat beneath her skin as she gently removed his mask, letting it fall to the floor as she gazed upon him, truly for the first time.

He was just as attractive as she knew he would be, and suddenly the voice and the boyish charm fit. He was breathtaking, a perfect design of timeless masculinity and innocence. His dark hair fell over his brow, those bright verdant eyes of his sharper against the contrast of his golden-kissed skin. Calliope's fingers trailed over his cheeks, down his jaw, over his lips. His hand hovered over the sides of her mask and she noticed the slight shake.

"May I?" he asked carefully. "Look at *you*?"

Calliope nodded without hesitation. "Yes." Her gaze implored him. "I think I would like that," she whispered.

He pushed her hair back and carefully removed her mask, and she didn't miss the glimmer of excitement, of hope in his gaze as he did so. He let out a heavy sigh, saying nothing for a moment as he stared at her, and Calliope started to worry something was wrong.

His gaze held hers as he finally

spoke.

"You are so fucking beautiful. I knew you would be, but..."

It certainly wasn't the first time a man or a woman had praised Calliope's eternal youth. The words shouldn't have lit her up the way they did, but it was the way Theo said them. Like a prayer.

"So are you," she whispered with a soft smirk as she reached out and trailed her fingertips along his jaw, over his plump lips, down his chest. They moved of their own volition, tracing the shape of his exquisite form.

I bet he would look beautiful spread over a chaise, cast in shadow and light.

She felt the faintest tingle in her fingertips, a familiar energy pooling in her core, in her heart.

And then she moved her fingertips

across his prominent bulge, sucking in a breath of her own as she felt the rigidity of his arousal.

Theo once more made no move to push her or grind against her like she expected him to. Instead, he waited. Patiently. And it was at that moment, Calliope realized he was nervous, waiting for her assurance, her guidance. Her lead.

And that realization in itself was rather inspiring.

"Tell me what you want, Calliope," he whispered once more, imploring her gaze as his hands slid over her bra carefully. He trailed his fingertips over the smooth cups, his thumbs brushing the cool fabric, making her nipples twitch beneath the surface.

In all her years, with all her patrons,

all the flames of her life, not one man or woman had ever asked Calliope what *she* wanted.

There were a hundred things she could have told Theo, but the thought of baring her soul the way she truly wanted to, even now, was too much. Though she did want to tell him the truth, she feared that telling this man such things would only break her heart in the process because she knew he couldn't give her what she truly wanted.

No one could.

But perhaps it was the alcohol, or the way he was looking at her, or perhaps it was the spark inside of her that refused to die in his presence, but whatever it was, she blamed it for the words that fell out of her mouth next.

"I want you to worship me," she

whispered. "On your knees."

There was a heavy pause as the words hung in the air between them, and for a moment she thought perhaps she'd said too much, demanded too much. She knew better than to *ask* for anything. From anyone. But Theo only smirked, the shadows cast from the overhead light above them lighting up his expression like a demon.

His deep phthalo gaze warmed her cheeks and just as Calliope thought he was going to push her back against the bed and make some adorably awkward quip, he dropped to his knees. Just like she demanded. Flashing those vibrant eyes up at her, she could not refute the sight was far more seductive than it should have been. A slight gasp escaped her throat as she reveled in the way he simply obeyed her. Without question, without protest.

Anything you want.

She opened her legs without question and Theo slid his hands up and over her ass, pulling her toward him with a heavy force. Calliope stumbled a bit from the motion, but stopped when she felt his fingers hooking into the side of her panties. He pushed them aside, sliding one finger into her heated entrance, and she nearly yelped from the sensation that accosted her. It was startling, warm, and heavy and made her gasp for breath.

Calliope looked down to see Theo, his face flush with her sex, and she didn't miss the way he used his free hand to squeeze his covered cock before returning his hand to her hip. Her heart fluttered, knowing it was because of *her*.

Knowing she had such an effect on him, the perfect human. It fed her spark in a way she'd never felt before. Seeing this beautiful man on his knees was... intoxicating.

"As you wish, Princess," he said darkly. His gaze held hers as he slowly started to pump his finger in and out of her slick entrance while his thumb flicked at her clit and relief flooded her. But it was only momentary relief, as it always was.

For his touch wasn't enough. Nothing would ever be *enough*. But for tonight at least, Calliope rationalized she could enjoy the brief respite of warmth and hope the spark gave her, for however long it lasted.

The spark Theo gives me. Because I

know in the morning, this will all fade.

It always fades. Nothing lasts forever. No matter how badly we wish it could.

Before Calliope could latch on to the thought, she felt the warmth of his lips on her. His fingers slowly continued to stroke her, his thumb massaging her as he took her clit into his mouth and sucked. Hard. The groan that escaped him was like music to her ears.

Calliope's eyes fell shut without hesitation and her entire body relaxed. Her fingers found his hair and Calliope embraced the softness as she tightened her grip on his locks, gently pushing him closer. It had been too long since she'd felt such pleasure. Perhaps she'd missed it more than she thought...

Or perhaps it is that I never knew what I was truly missing, because Theo's mouth is truly wicked.

The spark inside of her grew as she slowly started to grind herself against his mouth, his muffled moans and groans echoing in the space between them. His tongue slipped in alongside his fingers and her orgasm hit her like a lightning bolt.

"Oh Gods, Theo..." she yelped, her legs starting to shake as the onslaught pushed forth. Calliope steeled her grip on Theo's hair, if only to keep from falling as the wave of pleasure hit her. In all the years she'd been on this Earth, she had never come so *quickly.*

She expected Theo to stop now that he'd reached his goal, in favor of reaching his own, but he did no such thing. Instead, he kept *going,* a deep moan escaping him as he continued to lave and lick at Calliope's pussy, his fingers curling inside of her, stroking her sensitive insides. Her knees buckled and she nearly went down again, knocking both of them over.

Pull yourself together, Callie!

Theo chuckled, the sound making more than her insides tingle as he slid his fingers out of her, kissing her swollen bud before looking back up at her. Calliope's cheeks heated at the sight of his lustful gaze, his mouth and chin glistening with the evidence of his victory. And then he grabbed Calliope by her thighs and upended her onto her back in one fell swoop onto the floor.

Calliope cried out in surprise.

"I like when you scream my name," he said with a smirk as he angled himself on top of her, his caged hardness pressing against her heated mound. The spark, the energy inside her, all around her, between *them* flared to life with renewed vigor.

Theo leaned on his elbows beside her, regaling her with a cocky gaze that was equal parts sexy and challenging. "I think I want to hear you do it again," he said between his heated kiss, so full of hunger.

Calliope could taste herself on his tongue and she didn't hate it. Not one bit.

Well, that's...new.

Calliope lifted her hips, angling to meet his solid cock, her body craving *more.* The spark had caught, as it always did in the heat of the moment, and the line where Calliope began and her spark ended started to blur.

"Theo..." she breathed his name, trying to find the words she longed to say, but it was like her brain had short-circuited.

Theo's lips traveled down her neck, his hands freeing her breasts from their cups. The cool air made her skin pebble with goosebumps, her nipples stiff and sensitive. His tongue bathed her peaked nipples in warmth as he nibbled, kissed, and sucked them, in similar fashion to his treatment of her pussy. And all at once, Calliope felt that excitement, that familiar feeling culminating on the horizon. She moaned because words seemed to escape her at the moment.

Theo chuckled against her breast, pulling one nipple between his teeth gently as he used his free hand to pull and pinch the other.

"I'm going to come," Calliope managed to choke out, her voice high-pitched and strained. Her legs were still shaking, her insides so sensitive she feared another orgasm would render her numb.

The realization that she was indeed going to come again hit her quite hard, and she felt rather conflicted. She wanted more, but she was not sure she could take it. She hadn't experienced multiple orgasms since she'd been with Chuck.

She closed her eyes, forcing the thought out of her brain. She did not want to think of the pegacorn ever, and especially not at this moment, with Theo driving her to the brink of pleasure once more. And because Theodore was quite insistent on giving her such pleasure—

judging by his prominent hardness, it was safe to assume he was enjoying this as much as she was, and that itself was a turn on for Calliope.

"Theo," she cried, her entire body starting to shake as she braced for the oncoming wave of pleasure. Again.

Every nerve in her body felt strung like a tight wire and her muscles ached, her body hot as sweat formed beneath her breasts, among other places.

Theo ground his cock against her hesitantly, the smooth fabric of his briefs cool to the heat of her exposed flesh. His mouth latched onto her nipple and continued his appraisal of her breast with his tongue. And once again, without warning, Calliope's entire body unraveled like a spool of thread.

Theo disappeared between her legs

once again, his mouth kissing and sucking at her clit again, his tongue sliding inside of her, and she cried out because everything felt so *heightened.*

But her spark grew like a wildfire in a brittle forest.

Theo looked up at Calliope from his spot between her legs and she noticed his hand on his covered cock once more.

"Tell me what *you* want, Theodore," she whispered, her voice shaky as a fresh bout of moisture bloomed between her legs, but she was not sure if it was from his mouth or the sight of him like this.

Hard. Needy.

"Tell me and I will give it to you," she whispered, her words an echo of a familiar sentiment. It wasn't the first time she'd said them, and she knew this wouldn't be the last, either.

It seemed the tables had turned.

Calliope knew it was easier to give than *take*. She had never been a greedy woman, but perhaps that was truly her curse. What separated her from the gods and goddesses. As badly as she wanted to be praised, she *liked* praising others. As badly as she wanted to be worshipped and adored, she needed a human to worship and adore to feel inspired, herself. The balance was never quite equal, though.

But her desire to *give* Theo the pleasure he had given her was beyond craving. It was a desperate need.

I need to please him. I need to feel the spark he ignites within me...

He looked at her with hazy eyes, licking his lips.

CALLIOPE

Calliope sat up, the motion driving him back and further from her pulsing core. She ached for his sweet, wicked mouth, knowing what it was capable of, but she pushed the thought aside. She had taken *enough.* It was time to give her darling little chipmunk the treat he deserved.

Because no matter what he asked of her, Calliope vowed she would give him what he wanted. And he would take it the same way everyone else did. Without hesitation. She would give him the spark he needed, and then he would leave her. And with that spark, he'd do something wonderful, magnificent, and she would never know. And in time, she would fade from his memory. Become nothing but a story, a tale of his youth.

He'll forget my name, but he'll never

forget the spark I gave him.

But I will remember it all. I will remember his cocky assertion of likening drinks to personalities. I will remember his phthalo green patinae eyes and his wicked tongue. I will remember his perfect, golden Adonis body, and the fire he ignited within me for one, perfect night.

Calliope reached for his hand, the one covering his cock. She pushed his hand away, and he let her. Her fingertips grazed over the head of his cock, feeling the faint wetness against the fabric of his briefs.

"I want to make you come again," he said, his voice dark and thick with lust.

Calliope sauntered over him, pushing him until he fell over, his back hitting the bottom left foot of her easel and knocking some paint tubes onto the floor. She didn't let up, though, as she positioned herself over his cock, slipping her fingers through the hole in his briefs.

Theo tensed.

"If you want me to stop, I'll stop." she told him. She needed him to trust her, trust that she *could* give him the pleasure he deserved. He hadn't asked for anything. Even when he offered to buy her a drink, he did not ask for one in return. He did not ask to take her home to his place. And even after two leg-shattering orgasms, he had not once asked Calliope to touch him, to taste him. She was not certain *why* he was holding back. Or what he was afraid of.

Unless I am not what he truly wants...

She froze at the thought.

"No," he shook his head. "I don't want you to stop, I just—"

Calliope slowly wrapped her hand around his cock, slipping her hand inside his briefs, feeling the size of him. He filled her hand perfectly, her insides aching to know what he felt like, how he tasted. How he would feel stretching her with his cock.

But this wasn't about *her.*

"Is this what you want?" she asked, squeezing him lightly before she tugged down his briefs.

He gently lifted his hips, allowing her to remove his briefs completely, his eyes falling shut as his cock bobbed free. The glistening arousal pebbling his cockhead caught the light, and Calliope had to stop for a moment to appreciate the sight before her.

Theo and his dark hair all mussed, his golden form and perfectly defined muscles. Surrounded by tubes of paint on her bedroom floor, his sizeable cock springing free, one sticky, clear string of precum sticking to his thigh.

Calliope straddled his legs, grasping his cock in her hand. Her fingers gently caressed the spot over his leaking slit and he groaned, his body shuddering.

"No," he whispered.

Calliope leaned down, swiping her tongue across his cockhead, tasting his sweetness, detecting just a hint of juicy, sweet pineapple among the saltiness. He let out a deep groan, his hand finding her hair, and he stroked it reverently.

"Is this what you want?" Calliope asked, sucking the sweet juice from his tip.

He nodded vehemently. "Yes," he breathed, huskily.

Calliope smiled. "Your wish is my command," she muttered as she took his cock into her mouth slowly.

"Oh fuck, Callie..." Theo cried out, and then her spark truly ignited, awakening a part of her she'd never known before.

CHAPTER FOUR

THE MINUTE CALLIOPE wrapped her mouth around Theo's cock, he saw stars. Literally.

Theo looked up at the ceiling, noting the galaxy painted there, the bright, shimmering stars like grounding beacons.

He had never been the kind of guy who asked for things. Especially sexual things. He'd always preferred to be *told* explicitly what to do. There was less room for error that way. If he was doing what a woman asked him to do, he could guarantee her satisfaction. And not ruin the moment with his overly sensitive cock.

He cried out, partly in frustration and partly in euphoria, because Callie barely got his cock halfway in her mouth before he came without warning.

"Oh fuck," he groaned, mortification hitting him like a tidal wave.

Shit, that was too fast... even for me.

He expected her to pop off, now that she had reciprocated, because usually that's how it went for Theo, and the sadness and guilt had already started to fester, but Calliope didn't make a move to leave his cock. Instead, she kept sucking and stroking him, her little moans and sounds escaping her throat making it seem as if she actually *liked* this.

And that made Theo's insides warm with heat, his heart beating a little faster. Fear and lust culminated, because he knew if she didn't stop, he might come again, which wouldn't be terrible, but in Theo's experience, that was not always a good thing. The words of his exes judging him tried to poison his brain, but he shoved their words away. He didn't want to think about them, not with Miss Perfect and her warm, sweet mouth wrapped around his cock.

And then she stopped, suddenly, and he opened his eyes. Her gaze caught his and then he *felt* her.

Everywhere.

Or more accurately her soaked pussy,

sliding over his still-hard cock, and Theo couldn't help the moan that escaped him. She was so wet and smooth and he didn't think he'd ever felt anything like this before in all his life.

He was riding off the sugary sweet pleasure Callie was delivering to him, off the energy that ebbed between them.

This... this wasn't just sex. It was heaven, and Theo didn't want to let it go.

Let go. The little voice in his head whispered. *Give in.*

Except, Theo feared that giving in would be his undoing. Which didn't make any sense to him.

"Is this what you want?" she asked, her voice smooth and warm. He could feel the edge of her panties, bunched to the side.

"Not like this." He gently pushed

Calliope off of him, shaking his head, not missing her soft whimper as he did so. She sounded almost sad. Theo slid one hand between them, hooking his fingers into the sides of her panties, and pushed them down her thighs.

Calliope shimmied out of them, the movement pressing Theo into the ground, and he leaned back onto some bumpy tubes of paint once more, but he did not seem to care at the moment. Everything around him was white noise. There was only *her*. Calliope. Callie. Miss Perfect.

He settled his hands on her thighs once more, before using one hand to find his aching cock. His gaze captured hers as he spoke. "I don't want anything between us."

Calliope's eyes glowed once more, but

this time they were not gold or amber. They glowed a deep, undulating *purple* for a flicker of a moment. And then they returned to normal. Theo had never seen anything like it, and he was certain he was hallucinating.

"Then nothing will come between us," Calliope's smooth voice promised.

Something about the words felt deep, rooted in something Theo could not quite explain. Calliope's hand settled on his chest as she leaned down to kiss him, angling herself over him once more. The tip of his cock brushed her entrance, and he did not hesitate to guide himself into his Princess's pussy once more, this time without any barriers. His entrance was quick, the combination of her warmth and her kiss were too much to resist and so Theo gave in without a fight. He kissed her deeply, rocking his hips into her slowly as he relished the feel of her around him, like this.

His thumb found access to her clit again, and she groaned.

She seems to really like this, he thought, noting the way her body responded to his touch. No woman had ever responded to his touch quite like Callie, and he wasn't sure if it was him, the alcohol, or the heat of the moment. Perhaps a cocktail of all three. Whatever it was, Theodore felt as if he was flying higher than the sky.

Drinks or no drinks, he would never forget this moment. This blissful moment when everything was *perfect.*

He rocked his hips slowly, trying to ground himself to the here and now, for he didn't want to get carried away so quickly. He feared coming too soon, ruining the moment. He let Calliope set the pace, getting lost in the feel of her hands on his chest, her insides clenching him tightly.

Theo flashed his gaze up at her, his words nearly breathless as he spoke without a second thought. "You're so perfect," he whispered, reaching for her hair. His fingers settled in the locks as he pulled her to his lips once more, trying to make her understand something he could barely grasp himself.

Theo did not understand the spark catching inside of him. He did understand that fate had divined him to this very moment, that everything in his short twenty-four years of life had been leading him here. To her.

To Calliope.

Calliope kissed him as she pulled him up from the ground and he followed her wordlessly. The motion drove him deeper inside of her and he couldn't help but groan from the heightened sensation. His legs felt numb, his body was hot like a volcano and his hips moved of their own accord, relishing in the sharp pleasure.

Theo moved suddenly, like a man possessed. The energy between them erupted into blissful chaos as he gave into the spark inside of him, abandoning all thoughts of cautious hesitation and holding back. His reciprocation was more than assurance, it was perfection. It was a promise.

Calliope's breaths turned rapid as she met his hard thrusts, their bodies bathed in sweat and fire. Theo had never felt so good. So inspired. The world was his oyster, now that he'd found her.

"God, you feel so fucking good," he muttered against her shoulder, slowly thrusting into her.

Calliope's eyes fell shut. "So do you," she whispered.

Theo held on to her body with a possession, a desire that was an entity all its own. He never wanted to let go of this. To let go of *her.*

He groaned as she thrust herself against him. "It's like you were made for my cock." He could not control the words coming out of his mouth, but for the first time, he didn't *want* to. Honesty felt good. It was freeing.

"Like you were made to be *mine.*"

The word struck him in the chest as Calliope gasped.

"Say that again," she pleaded.

"What?" he asked, his voice hazy. His thrusts slowed. He could hear the edge in his voice as his insides swirled with heat and desire and something else he could not place.

"That I'm *yours*," she said, her voice faint and pleading.

Theo knew he could not deny her. Ever.

Nor did he want to. He wanted to give Calliope *everything.*

Theo's lips brushed her ear softly as he thrust himself into her, wanting to bury himself there forever.

"You're *mine*, Calliope." He brushed his lips over the shell of her ear.

Calliope's eyes fluttered from the praise, her insides clenching him like a hurricane.

His balls drew tight, his stomach clenched, and he knew it wouldn't be long until his inevitable orgasm would take hold. But even as badly as he wanted to give into the pleasure, he wanted it to last forever, too. But nothing lasted forever, least of all amazing, mind-blowing sex. Which Theo had never had until this moment.

He stilled, trying to hold back his pleasure, not because he wanted it to stop, but because he was a gentleman, and did not want to take away from Callie's experience.

"Please don't stop," she whined, and he could hear the ecstasy in her voice. "Theo—"

"But I want you to come first," he said, licking his lips. He opened his eyes, imploring her with his gaze.

There was a strange tightness in his chest as fear and guilt hit him, though he wasn't sure why.

His voice was strained. He needed her to understand, but how could he make her understand something he did not? His mind was jumbled with words and phrases and thoughts that made no sense. His memories of Emily tried to bleed into perfection, her annoyance at how quickly he came, or the fact he refused to have sex without a condom. The bitterness in her voice as she pushed him aside angrily melded with the memory of his proposal and his discovery of her cheating. But there was also the sweetness of Calliope's laugh in the cafe, her alluring smile and her perfect, pineapple-flavored kiss.

There was a warmth in his chest as

his words reverberated in his brain, promising the woman *anything she wanted.* Those words danced with the word *forever* and *worship* and *mate.* Nothing made sense to him as the hurricane inside of him built itself, sweeping up everything Theo was and knew in its path.

And as he looked in Calliope's amber eyes, he understood this was everything.

Because she was the center of *everything.*

She was his. Now and *forever.*

Forever...

He tried to find the right words, but between his culminating orgasm and the chaos in his brain, all that came out of his mouth was, "I need you to come first..."

Theo grit his teeth, closing his eyes as

he tried to hold off his orgasm like a knight with a wooden sword trying to hold off a dragon.

Callie's comforting voice beckoned him like a lamb to the slaughter.

"Theo, look at me..." she whispered.

The guilt and shame hit him all at once. He could not look at her, for fear of the sympathy, the judgment that would be there, because he was far too close to the edge and he knew he would fail Calliope just as he had Emily. He would never be enough. He was not going to be able to get her there at this point, like he wanted to. Like she deserved.

His oversensitive cock was going to ruin everything. Again.

The words of his past swirled to the surface, threatening to take him under.

I told you not to come yet!

CALLIOPE

Why can't you wait? What's wrong with you?

Again Theo?

You need to learn how to control yourself.

Callie's movements slowed down, but she didn't stop. She slowly rode him, her fingertips trailing over his chest softly before she wrapped her arms around his neck. Each thrust became another shattering crack to the breaking glass holding Theo together.

She grabbed his jaw with one hand, her voice warm and smooth and too hard to fight.

"Theodore, look at *me*."

Theo opened his eyes, finding her amber ones gazing back at him, and a jolt of energy ricocheted through him like lightning, lighting up every nerve, every vein in his body. His vision flickered violet for only a split second, a trick of the light he garnered.

In her gaze, he could see his reflection. There, he noted the desperation, the need etched in his own.

He hated it.

But the way Calliope was looking at *him* told him she didn't. Not one bit.

Hunger blossomed inside of him, awakening like a monster from hibernation.

"You said I am *yours*. That I could have whatever I want. Did you not?" Her voice was like a lullaby, tempting and comforting. He nodded.

"Yes." He did not miss the way his voice shook. "Anything," he murmured.

Her thumb stroked his jaw before sliding over his lips. "I want *you* to come,

Theo. For me." Her words were solid, unwavering. It wasn't a request, it was a command.

Something switched inside Theo, perhaps the lock on his monster's cage. For Calliope's words were like a spell, a promise, a balm to his soul. He knew he should not trust her so easily, in the back of his mind, he knew this. He knew that he was dancing on a tightrope, and something told him it was about to snap. But for the first time in his life, Theo felt like perhaps if he fell, he'd be all right. Because someone would catch him.

Calliope would catch him.

"I want you to come *with me*," she whispered against his lips.

Theo's breath hitched in his throat. He could barely breathe. He nodded as tears fell down his cheeks. Her command was more freeing than either of them could understand at the moment.

The words fell out of his mouth of their own volition. "As you wish, Princess." His voice sounded strange, even to his own ears. He kissed Calliope, hard, and his body loosened as he let go, giving in to her demand, freeing the monster and the hurricane inside of him with one hard thrust.

Theo's orgasm hit him like a brick to the stomach as he unraveled inside her.

Every bone in his body turned to Jell-O. His muscles felt liquefied. Energy barreled through him, lighting him up like a display of fireworks. The tightness in his chest spread dand it was like he had become someone else.

Yet despite the numbness in his

limbs, the energy spurred him forth like an adrenaline rush as he lunged forward, upending Calliope once more onto the hardwood floor beneath them. Paint spattered from the tubes beneath them, staining their skin shades of red and green and purple and everything in between.

Calliope wrapped her legs around Theo's waist as he continued his thrusts into her, riding out the tidal wave of pleasure that felt more freeing than anything he'd ever felt before. He wanted to drown in it.

And for the briefest moment, that is what Theo did. He lost himself in everything. Her kiss, her warmth, her touch, even the cool paint against his flesh as her body moved, spreading it like ivy along abandoned brick walls. He didn't know where he began, or where she ended. All he knew was that one word that kept repeating in his brain. The one that made no sense.

Mate.

Something inside him longed to say it. But instead, he said, "All mine."

"All yours," Calliope whispered as she came undone around him.

And as she did so, Theo could have sworn the earth was quaking beneath them.

Calliope's voice was breathless. "Good boy," she whispered.

Theo let out a heavy sigh, his entire body melting into Calliope's warmth. He thought perhaps he was dreaming.

Because those words settled *everything* inside of him.

All yours.

CALLIOPE

Good boy.

Theo let out a sigh of relief as he kissed her again. They rolled onto their side, legs and arms clutching one another, spreading paint and desire along their bare skin like a masterpiece. When their lips broke apart, and Theo removed himself from Calliope's warmth, the world shifted on its axis. Or at least, that was how it felt for Theodore as he pulled her close, as he collapsed onto his back, his wet cock falling against his stomach, leaving trails of moisture along his skin. Calliope curled close to him, resting her head on his chest, and he held her close to his side as the darkness took them both past the point of no return.

CHAPTER FIVE

THE SOUND OF heavy banging roused Calliope from her slumber with a groan. Her head was pounding, her shoulder and neck aching something fierce, and her body felt strangely clammy and warm and weighted down.

Good grief, how much alcohol was in those bloody drinks last night?

Her eyelashes fluttered as she filtered in the light streaming through her windows, her vision a blur of colors that felt more Monet than Mondrian. A groan beside her pulled her attention as she sat up, and the heaviness fell from her chest, down her abdomen, landing in her lap.

She rubbed her eyes as her vision sharpened, the light of late morning illuminating the scene in front of her.

Paint tubes strewn about the floor, dried acrylic sticking to the floorboards in puddles, clothes lining the pathway from the door. A plastic, black mask that had been crushed, stained with bright cadmium red paint.

And then the sound beside her deepened, the weight in her lap sliding between her thighs, and all at once Calliope remembered precisely what happened. Flashes of Zorro—no, *Theodore*—permeated in her psyche. His perfect kiss, his deep voice promising her *anything she wanted.* His wicked mouth driving her into oblivion not once, but twice. His cock filling her.

She turned in earnest, panic and anxiety culminating inside of her as she looked at Theo—naked, spatters of paint covering his golden skin like a Jackson Pollack painting.

Her heart climbed into her throat as she remembered him on his knees. Her words to him a spell all their own.

I want you to worship me.

What was she thinking? How had she let herself be so... so... open?

"So loud," he murmured groggily, tugging her hip with his hand.

All mine.

His words reverberated in her brain.

The loud banging on the door

continued, getting louder, faster.

"Callie! Wake up!" An aggravated, high-pitched voice called out, one quite familiar.

"Will you stop yelling!" It was hard not to recognize Spike's—Hecate and Hades's former cursed hellhound shifter who had recently found his mate in her friend and former student, Izzy—deep and sophisticated voice, even from rooms away, and Calliope sat up straighter. Izzy and Spike were not ones to bother her at home. Especially on a weekend.

Theo groaned, rubbing his eyes and his forehead. "What the hell is all the yelling?"

Calliope leapt up from the floor, her nerves frayed as she tried to figure out which fire to put out first, though her head was pounding and her body felt too cramped and achy from the fact she'd slept on the floor... with Theodore.

Oh my Gods.

Theo sat up as she sprung toward her door.

"Callie..." he murmured, his voice groggy but also carrying a hint of alarm.

But she could not answer him right now. She could not focus on Theo at all, only the incessant loud shouting and heavy fists on her door. She threw on her pink kimono robe, cinching and tying it as fast as she could as she padded across the floor to her door, not stopping to look back at the man she'd left on the floor in her bedroom like a shredded piece of decoupage.

"Callie! God, I swear if you're lying dead in there, I'm going to kill you!" Izzy screamed just as Calliope reached the door and hurriedly unlocked it, throwing it open.

On the other side of the door stood Izzy, dressed in a *Monster F*cker* t-shirt and black jeans and boots, her blonde hair disheveled, sticking out in all sorts of directions as if she, too, had risen from a dead sleep. Spike stood beside her, his dark hair also equally messy, but he looked a bit more put together with his black jeans, white shirt, and matching leather jacket. His eyes widened as he took in the sight of Calliope, whose head was practically splitting.

"What are you raving on about?"

Izzy did not waste a second as she rushed indoors, entering Calliope's humble abode and Spike sighed as Izzy started her debriefing.

"Spike and I thought we'd get to the fucking gallery *early* you know, so like... we could clock out a little bit early and check out the show over at *Bandwidth* later this evening and—"

"Slow down, Isabelle," Calliope said as she hurried after the vampire, Spike sighing in exhaustion as he chased the rambling vampire as well.

Izzy threw her hands up in the air. "Would you just listen?"

"I'm trying," Calliope said as Izzy headed straight for her kitchen, making a beeline to her coffee pot.

Isabelle and Lorelai had visited her on occasion, mostly when they wanted to borrow a brush or paint, or possibly even submit extra credit outside of lecturing hours, so it wasn't as if

Calliope was bothered by her friend's level of comfort in her home on a regular day, but today was certainly not a *regular* day for Calliope. Not by a long shot.

"Where the fuck is the coffee?" Izzy huffed. "You *always* have coffee."

Calliope sighed as she pushed past Isabelle and headed for the cabinet to grab her coffee filters and grounds as Spike chimed in.

"I think what Iz is trying to say is—"

"If you would stop interrupting me, and let me talk—" Izzy huffed as Calliope felt her pulse rising.

"Spike? What the hell are you doing here?"

Calliope stopped mid coffee ground pour, as Theo's voice permeated through the air. It was like the world froze and her legs had turned to stone.

"Theo?" Spike's surprised tone fell on her ears and she had to remember to *breathe.* Because Spike said his name.

"Who the hell are you?" Izzy asked, her tone slightly judgmental.

Calliope sucked in a breath as she turned slightly to see Theo, breathing a sigh of relief as she noticed he was dressed. Haphazardly, with his blue button-down half hanging out of his black dress paints, his sleeves half rolled and undone, his hair sticking out every which way.

"Theo was my lab partner in bio last semester," Spike muttered.

"How do you know Callie?" Theo asked, and Calliope could hear an edge of something sharp in his voice. Jealousy or anger, or... possession?

No, that would be silly, that would mean—

"She was my Painting 101 instructor last semester."

"For the love of all things holy, can we do meet and fucking greets another time!" Izzy huffed as Calliope blinked, coming back to the here and now, starting the coffee pot as fast as she could before she stuck two fingers in her mouth and whistled. Loudly.

The *students* in her midst ceased their squabbling, all turning to look at her.

"Isabelle, please. What are you and Spike doing here at—" She checked her wall clock, noting the time was nearing almost noon. She—and Theodore—had slept nearly nine, ten hours almost.

She'd never slept so long in all her

life! And this certainly wasn't her first hangover.

"Eleven thirty-eight in the morning?"

Izzy rolled her eyes. "That's what I was trying to say! Spike and I were headed to the Gallery—"

"The Leehan Gallery?" Theo asked, as they all turned to look at him.

"Is there, like... another gallery on campus?" Izzy bit as Calliope pinched the bridge of her nose.

"There is not. Izzy, please get to the point—"

"Are you hung over?" Spike asked, the innocence in his voice almost comical. Though Spike may have looked like a man who could murder you and not blink an eye, he was far from dangerous or murderous. He'd only just become human again after nearly a century, and was still learning how to navigate the modern world. With Izzy by his side, and his friends, which included Calliope.

And apparently, Theodore.

What were the odds?

"Spike—"

"Anyway, as I was *trying* to say," Izzy huffed as the coffee spat ominously, "Spike and I went early to check out all the shit on the schedule for the new work study joining the shit show—"

Theo raised his hand, and Calliope felt as if her head was going to explain.

"Theodore..."

"Um... am I supposed to come in today or something?"

"What are you talking about?" Callie bit.

"The Leehan... Gallery... that's... my

work study this semester."

Calliope felt the blood drain from her body at his words.

"I'm sorry, what—"

"The Leehan Gallery... it was all I could fit into my schedule this year, and... uh... how did you know I was *here*?" Theo asked curiously, his eyebrows furrowing.

Spike raised an eyebrow. "We didn't. We're not here for *you*."

"What does Callie have to do with the gallery?" he asked.

Izzy huffed in annoyance as the coffee pot beeped. She grabbed the pot as Calliope tried to focus on her breathing.

Her shoulders felt heavy, the world moving at the speed of sound around her, and she was starting to think she may explode.

She was not equipped enough to handle all of this with a hangover, an achy back, and short patience.

"Callie works at the gallery, duh. She's our boss."

Theo let out a nervous half-laugh as his verdant gaze met hers. He looked like he'd seen a ghost.

"Callie is... the manager of the gallery?"

Spike nodded. "I mean, she's faculty and Brian's right hand since he took over so—" Spike said as Izzy poured herself a cup of coffee, not bothering to offer anyone else a mug.

She continued her spiel. "Can we focus here? Yes, Callie is the manager of the gallery. No we're not here for you—" Isabelle regarded Theo with a judgmental look before gazing back at

Calliope.

"We're here because when we got there, the gallery was already open... sort of."

"What do you mean, sort of?" Calliope asked, noting that Theo had gotten marginally closer than she had realized. She shifted out of his space, feeling equal parts anxious and vulnerable.

Theodore was a *student*. And not just any student, but *her* student. A student who would be working underneath her in the gallery.

Calliope had patrons from all walks of life, but in the time she'd been attending and working at the university, she'd never taken a *student* as a patron. For starters, the idea felt icky to her. Calliope did not prefer to be in positions of power over her patrons. Her job was simply to give, to support. Not to command.

And she certainly didn't feel right getting involved with a student in *her* wheelhouse.

But the truth was unavoidable at that moment.

She hadn't known who Theo was, and he hadn't known who she truly was, either. But now that she *knew*, it was not something she could forget.

She did not want to take advantage of her student, her *employee*. It was a line she had never crossed, and she wasn't certain she wanted to now, of all times. No matter how perfect Theodore's kiss was, or how he'd made her feel.

I knew this was a mistake...

Gods, I have really done it this time.

"Well, when we got to the gallery, the

doors were unlocked, and they were wide open," Spike said carefully.

"Did you forget to *lock* them?" Calliope challenged.

Izzy sipped her coffee, shaking her head, the motion making her golden hair sway back and forth. "Nope, Spike said he and Lora triple checked it last night. Those doors were definitely locked," Izzy said.

"So obviously we checked the displays and everything to make sure everything was accounted for, and that's when—" Spike wrung his hands nervously.

Calliope felt a sinking feeling in her stomach as she looked between Spike and Isabelle.

"Everything was... accounted for... right?" Calliope asked, her voice shaking.

Spike shook his head. "No, Callie, I'm afraid something was missing."

Calliope closed her eyes, sucking in a breath as she tried to focus. "What was missing, Spike?"

But it was Isabelle who answered. "The diviner was missing."

Calliope felt her knees buckle from the weight of the words. But before she could fall to the ground, she felt warm, steady hands at her hips, holding her still. Even with her eyes closed, she knew she would recognize that touch anywhere.

It would be impossible to forget.

She opened her eyes to see Theo, his eyebrows furrowed, those deep green pools imploring her gaze. The desire to get lost and fall into them was prevalent, but she did not have time for such things. Not when the gallery had been burglarized, not when the object of such desires was her newest employee.

So she pushed Theo's hands off of her and backed away, toward Spike.

"You are sure?" she turned to him, giving Theo her back.

Spike nodded, meeting her gaze. "Positive."

Calliope took a deep breath, turning to Isabelle. "And you are certain that *only* the diviner is missing?"

Isabelle nodded. "Yeah. We checked, believe me."

"All right, did you alert Brian?" Calliope tried her best to remain calm, though it felt as if she was on the edge of a breakdown for sure.

There were plenty of things more

valuable in the gallery than the diviner—the crystal that was quite famous for showing one their divined mate—such as the ancient tablets and statues carved from much more precious stones, not to mention the gold and silver jewelry Professor Leehan—Brian, the current owner's father who was in his retirement process—had salvaged on his last excursion before his heart attack.

"No. We... uh, wanted to come to *you* first. Thought maybe you could help?" Spike pursed his lips. "I said we should tell him, but Izzy said—"

"No, no, you did the right thing," Calliope said, letting out a breath. "It's best not to alarm Brian yet until we know more about the situation. Have you checked the camera footage?"

Spike shook his head. "No. We came

straight here. I mean… we locked up and came straight here."

"Okay," Calliope moved toward the kitchen table and she could feel Theo's gaze on her. Moving with her.

"I, uh… need to get dressed, and then we can head over to the gallery and—" She stopped, looking up at Theo. "You should probably go home."

There was a tense silence as Theo's eyebrows furrowed, his expression faltering. He had the audacity to look hurt.

Calliope hated it, but perhaps it was better this way. She needed to put some distance between them. Least of all *now*. She knew one night of pure passion was not any sort of grounds for a relationship, and she didn't expect Theodore to be open to such things. She knew how these sorts of scenarios went, she'd been in them many times. She needed to rip the band-aid off. She needed to get to the gallery, figure out what happened to the diviner, and find a way to get it back before Brian found out.

Quite a task for her, but she'd been in much more precarious situations before.

Such as when Mars had found himself losing his powers and turning into a mortal, with only days to find an answer and a mate, or when Izzy had bitten Spike, in which her venom had poisoned him and nearly killed him.

And she'd found her way out of those situations, she could certainly figure out how to crack the case of the missing diviner. She just needed to think, and with Theodore Lange in her presence, she could not think.

She could barely even breathe.

"Yeah, I, uh... my friend's probably worried about me, I'll just... uh, call an Uber and—"

"I can give you a ride," Spike said, pulling all their attentions.

"I beg your pardon—" Calliope started.

"Oh, no, you don't have to do that, I—" Theo started, but Spike held his hand up.

"It's fine, really."

Calliope shook her head, the heat of the moment getting to her. She needed to move, to get out of her kitchen. She needed to breathe, a moment to process this... insanity.

"I need to go... change," she said matter of factly, not bothering to look at

Theo, for she did not want to see the hurt expression on his perfect face, knowing his frown would be her fault.

I'm such a fool! Damn you, Hattie! Damn you, DeLux Cafe! Damn Piña Coladas!

She did not look back at her guests, and instead, barreled forth out of the room and into her bedroom, all but slamming the door.

The moment she was behind it, she fell to the floor, her eyes nearly filling with tears as she pulled her knees to her chest, burying her face in her arms.

How had things become so complicated so quickly?

How had one perfect night turned into such an awful nightmare?

Not only was Theodore her employee and student, but the prized diviner had gone missing and the gallery had a thief on their hands.

The odds were stacking against Calliope, and she wasn't certain she wasn't truly cursed.

First David and now this... have I angered the gods or something? Why me? Why now?

She heard the door shut, and the moment it did, she felt an ache in her chest, an emptiness that hadn't been there a moment ago. She knew it was because he had left. Theo. She looked up, her gaze falling on the crumpled, paint-stained mask sitting in the center of the floor. It stared at her, vibrant and noticeable across the shiny black plastic.

He was gone, her Zorro. Her perfect stranger.

All yours, he said.

CALLIOPE

Calliope sighed, pushing the thought, the memory aside. She did not wish to think of their perfect moment, the moment where she felt truly *worshipped*. It could not happen again. She could not let it. She needed to remain professional. Distant. Inspiration or not, Calliope could not give in so easily. She needed to be better. She needed to protect herself. She needed to do *her* job.

And so she stood up, wiping her tears as she headed toward her dresser, picking out a skirt and blouse, and found herself a pair of low heels. She dressed quickly, running a brush through her hair and glazing some gloss over her lips before she opened the door.

Part of her hoped it had been an illusion, a mistaken sound, hoped that somehow, someway, Theodore would still be there. But when she opened the door, he wasn't there, and neither was Spike. There was only Izzy, sipping her coffee, her gaze fixed on Calliope as she raised her eyebrow at her.

Calliope sauntered toward Isabelle, not meeting her gaze. She headed for the key bowl by her door, not wishing to acknowledge the elephant in the room. And as they both piled into Calliope's Lincoln, there was a shared understanding. Izzy did not press her, and for that Calliope was grateful. But there was a part of her that wished her friend would press her. Ask her about what had happened, because Calliope wanted to talk about how *perfect* Theo was. How he'd driven her into orgasmic bliss and worshipped her with his mouth, his words, his *devotion.* But

CALLIOPE

Calliope vowed it would do no good truly, to discuss such things. It would only hurt her more. So she promised herself as she drove herself and Isabelle to the gallery, that she would do everything in her power to forget Theodore. Surely, it wouldn't be *that* difficult, right?

CHAPTER SIX

THERE WAS AN awkward silence as Theo got into the passenger side of Spike's sleek black BMW.

"Didn't peg you for a BMW guy," Theo murmured, trying his hardest to fill the silence, if only because he couldn't stand the tension.

"Hades, my—" Spike paused for a moment, as if he wasn't sure what to say. "Well, I guess he's kind of family but we're not related," he continued, "he has like a bunch of cars because he's collected them over the years and he doesn't really use more than one or two, so I guess he thought with me being in college, I'd probably need one, so..."

Theo nodded. "Must be nice having connections like that."

"I mean, I told him I was fine and I've been saving some cash from working at the gallery, but then when I went home to visit Cate... my, uh... she's kind of family, too, it was just there and she basically told me I couldn't send it back or she'd kick my ass, so..."

Theo laughed. "Hades, huh? Like the guy with the blue flame hair?"

Spike laughed, too. "I'm not sure I know what you mean."

Theo shrugged. "Nevermind."

The silence returned as Spike slowed

to a stop at a stop sign, turning to look at Theo.

"So... you and Callie..."

Theo felt his shoulders stiffen, suddenly on edge as Spike carefully spoke.

"How did you... uh ...meet?"

Theo shifted in his seat, feeling strangely on the spot. It wasn't as if Spike was being mean or pushy. In fact, it felt like a genuine question, but one framed with caution.

Like perhaps Spike felt something for Calliope, which made Theo feel all sorts of emotions he wasn't entirely ready to process.

He knew he could have shirked the question, changed the subject. But there was also a part of him that wanted to talk, to confide in someone. To vent, air out his thoughts. And Spike didn't seem like a terrible person. They'd spent a whole semester together as lab partners, and Theo couldn't deny that he was a rather decent partner, and he trusted him to do his work and carry his weight, so…

He could certainly trust him with this, couldn't he?

Theo carefully spoke. "Last night. Went out with my roommate and his friends to this place downtown, DeLux Cafe—"

"You're kidding," Spike said as he slowly picked up the gas.

Theo shrugged his head. "Nope. Last night they had some speed dating thing, a themed *Mystery Masquerade* or whatever, and my roommate, Trick, basically forced me to go because—" He stopped, unsure of how much to tell Spike. They'd been lab partners the previous semester, and he liked the guy enough, but he wasn't sure he wanted to divulge such personal details to an acquaintance. It wasn't like they hung out outside of class, and since said class had ended, he hadn't heard from Spike, nor did he expect to hear from him. Running into him in Calliope's kitchen was most serendipitous.

But the surprise of the moment paled to the reality of that morning.

When Theo had woken up, on the floor, his arms wrapped around a soft, warm body and the air smelled of vanilla, paint, and sex...

He'd barely had time to process what had happened before Calliope was shoving his arms off of her and tearing out the bedroom, as if she were trying to get as far away from him as she could. The burn was deep, as Theo's memories threatened to resurface. Memories of being discarded the morning after he'd had sex, post break up with Emily. He'd been drunk then, too. It was clear Tara, the woman Trick had tried to set him up with, had regretted sleeping with him. Judging by the way she looked at him the next morning, scoffed and said, "I'm never drinking tequila again."

And the second time...

The second time with Lyric, he was not drunk, but his oversensitive cock had ruined the evening, and as such, Lyric became offended and left. Which was precisely why Theodore had done his best to push aside his quest to find love as a twenty-something ex-fiancé, and focus on his studies. On the one thing he *was* good at.

But in the cases Theo had been rejected and regretted before, none stabbed him in the chest quite like Callie. For it wasn't *just* her fleeing the scene of the crime that had burned Theo, it was the ache he felt when she'd done so. He'd never felt as powerful as he had last night when she'd asked him to worship her, when she'd begged him to call her *his.*

And Theo was quite certain he'd never feel such power again. He'd watched her grab her robe and spring through the doorway, his heart in his throat.

He'd stayed frozen as she opened the door, a familiar voice along with one that was unfamiliar sounding in the space. A woman, who, by the sounds of it, had taken it upon herself to enter Calliope's humble abode.

Theo had been caught between mortifying discovery and curiosity. Who were these people gallivanting into Callie's apartment? And when Calliope's voice hitched with worry, Theo didn't think twice, for hearing her anxiety spurred him to move as fast as he could, if only so he could comfort her, soothe her.

His mate.

Even now the word in his brain was loud, evident, but it didn't make sense. Calliope was not his soulmate. There was no way one could discern such a thing from one night of drunk fooling around. Theo surmised if fate truly did exist—which he did not believe that it did—that it had never been on his side.

Yet, despite his qualms and confusingly muddled brain, he hurried into his clothes as fast as he could and found his way to Callie, who looked as if she was on the brink of a meltdown.

To comfort her was an instinctual response, and thus, he'd fallen into Callie's magnetic field without even noticing, seeking her flesh, wanting to touch, to soothe and provide her the spark of comfort he knew she needed.

But she had pushed him away. *Again.*

Perhaps he was wrong about Calliope the same way he'd been wrong about Emily or Tara or Lyric.

Perhaps Trick was wrong—Theo didn't have much to offer aside from his heart. And it seemed women didn't want

Theo's heart. They barely wanted his cock.

Theo did not finish his thought or his response to Spike, figuring it would be best to forget about what happened with Calliope. But how could he forget Miss Perfect? It didn't seem possible.

"Well, he just was trying to help, I guess. Get me outside my comfort zone and away from my books or whatever."

Spike nodded as they turned down the road leading to the dormitories.

"Right, I guess that makes sense," Spike said, twisting his lips.

"What?"

Spike slowed as he entered the parking lot, practically crawling in the lot.

"I really didn't mean to interrupt your... morning," Spike said evenly as he pulled into a parking space. For a moment, he did not turn the car off.

"It's fine, Spike, really. Don't worry about me," Theo said, reaching for the door just as Spike spoke up.

"I just..."

"What?" Theo asked in annoyance. "You keep looking at me like I'm about to catch fire or something, Spike. You're creeping me the fuck out."

Spike sighed, shaking his head as he opened his driver's side door. "I'm sorry, it's just... Callie... she's a friend. A really good friend, and she's been through a lot and I just... I guess I feel bad about the whole diviner thing."

Theo sighed as he followed suit, rounding the front of Spike's car until he was side by side with the man. Theo slid his hands in his pockets, the wind blowing his hair in the breeze.

Spike settled next to him, catching his gaze.

"I get it," Theo said, hanging his head. "She's kind of... amazing. Totally out of my league."

Spike walked beside him, his own hands in the leather pockets of his jacket.

"Obviously not, if you survived the night," Spike said with a smirk.

Theo couldn't help but chuckle, shaking his head. "Yeah, well, pretty sure the Piña Coladas are to blame for that, so I can't really take credit."

Spike's smile faltered as Theo shrugged.

"But enough about me and Callie, what, uh... what about the gallery?"

Spike and Theo walked slowly toward

Theo's dorm, passing several students going to and from their residences.

"What about it?"

"What's a... diviner?" Theo asked curiously.

Spike let out a breath. "How much do you know? About... Callie and the folks that attend DeLux's speed dates?"

Theo shrugged. "Not much, I guess. I mean, I just met her last night and my roommate and his friends are always raving about the drinks and—"

Spike looked uncomfortable as they headed toward the front door.

"What? Why do you keep looking at me like that?" Theo snapped as he threw open the door just as two girls exited, looking at him in judgment.

Spike followed after him. "Well, for starters you *reek* of muse."

CALLIOPE

What the fuck? Is this asshole telling me I stink? Who does that? That's so rude—

"Fuck you, too, Spike. You don't smell like a peach either, bud."

Theo wrinkled his nose at the fiery scent that always accompanied the man. It was like his cologne was forged in a fire or something, which wouldn't have been bad had it not been hot out and Theo was already feeling quite on edge.

"No, it's not... I mean..." Spike huffed out an annoyed sound as they stopped in the lounge. It was just the two of them. "There is probably no easy way to say this," Spike said with a sigh. "But, certain supernaturals have certain... scent markers."

Theo raised his eyebrow. "Supernaturals? Like vampires and

witches and shit?"

Spike nodded. "Emphasis on the shit. Think more like immortals. Gods, goddesses, shifters, and—" He licked his lips. "Immortal *Spirits*."

Theo shook his head. "Shit, don't tell me you're one of those guys like Trick and his friends who are into all that woo-woo marketing shit at the DeLux..."

Spike shook his head. "No, it's not woo-woo, and it's certainly not marketing. It's very real. That's how I met Izzy. Well, technically, I met her when I was in my other form—"

Theo raised an eyebrow. Spike was talking nonsense and he was starting to regret thinking Spike was a sane, normal guy. Clearly, he was losing his marbles...

"Other form? What are you, like, an alien or something?"

Spike narrowed his gaze seriously at Theodore. "No. I'm a hellhound."

It took everything in Theo to not laugh at the sincerity and seriousness in Spike's voice. It was as if he truly believed what he was saying.

A part of Theo wanted to refute such madness, but he couldn't deny there was a part of him that felt a strange warmth in his chest from the words.

Theo regaled him with a raised eyebrow.

"I know it sounds crazy, believe me, but it's the truth. I was literally cursed for a century as a hellhound until—Izzy—until she kind of forced my transition back because she's my mate."

The words were bonkers to Theo, but there was a truth in how Spike spoke that Theo couldn't ignore. Either the man was certifiably insane or Theo was still drunk from the previous night. The latter was unlikely, as he had the hangover to prove it.

Spike pursed his lips. "Izzy bit me, because she's a vampire and—"

Theo could not help but laugh as Spike's story seemed to be getting crazier by the minute.

"What's so funny?" Spike asked.

Theo shook his head. "You, Spike. You realize you sound bat shit insane right now."

Spike narrowed his gaze. "I know it must sound crazy, but it's the truth. And I think you know it is, you just don't want to acknowledge it."

Before Theo could respond, Spike implored his gaze with a serious one of his own.

"Izzy bit me, because she's a vampire, and if you remember, last semester when I was out for that big test in lab... well, it was because I was sick. Because she bit me and our *bond* wasn't complete."

"Vampires, Hellhounds, and bonds, oh my," Theo muttered as Spike crossed his arms.

"Izzy and I were fated mates. Just as Mars and Lorelai, and Cate and Gunner, and Hades and Darcy, and—"

Theo shook his head. "Spike, you're talking nonsense."

Spike pursed his lips once more. "The diviner is what showed *them* their bonds. It's an artifact, one Professor Leehan had uncovered and brought here, where it's been on display for the last six months, and now it's gone."

"So the thing that's missing is some kind of fate-diving artifact that tells you who you're going to marry or whatever?"

Spike's expression was stoic. "No one said anything about *marriage.*"

Theo scoffed, shaking his head. "Of course not." He turned away from Spike for a moment. "Don't you have to get back to the gallery or whatever? Look for this diviner?"

Spike nodded. "I do, but..."

Theo nodded toward the door. "Then you should probably go."

Spike looked between Theo and the door, before he spoke. "I should." His words were careful, steady. As if Spike himself felt obligation or guilt for the situation, even though it made no sense.

And something about that made Theo feel as if he'd gotten off on the wrong foot with Spike. With Calliope.

Who was next? Trick?

"Thanks for the ride," he said as he moved to head to the door that lead inside the building to the elevators.

Spike did not chase after him. He only said, "Five pm."

Theo turned to see Spike standing in the lobby, in the same spot he'd left him.

"What?"

"Iz and I work until four on Sundays. Callie usually comes in around two, stays until five to close up the gallery."

Spike twisted his lips as he shrugged. "Figured as the new work study, you might want to know the hours our *boss* keeps."

Spike's words settled on Theo. Calliope was *his boss.* Miss Perfect was the gallery manager. What were the odds?

Though Theo couldn't help but feel a spark of hope, despite knowing this truth. Callie may have been his boss, but she was still a person outside the gallery. A woman with desires and wants and needs, and they just *happened* to have this—the gallery—in common. That had to count for something, right?

"Okay, thanks for the heads up," Theo said as Spike headed for the door.

Theo spoke again, stopping him. "You, uh... still have my number?"

Spike turned and nodded. "I do. Why?"

"I mean, if you guys need any help later... or you have an update or something... you know, on what I'm supposed to do or... just, keep me posted?"

Spike gave him a reassuring smile. "Yeah, of course."

And with that, Spike left Theo alone once more.

When Theo had managed to make it up to his dorm room, he was surprised to see it was quiet and empty. No Trick, or Shaun, or anyone.

"Maybe they're just busy," he said out loud as he headed for his bedroom, figuring a hot shower and a long nap was just what he needed after his adventurous night and crazy morning.

His thoughts wandered to Spike's words as he undressed himself, heading for the bathroom. It was rare that he got time to himself at the dorm, what with Trick and his teammates often times occupying most of the dorm most of the time.

Theo slipped out of his briefs, stepping into the spray of the shower with ease, relishing in the warmth of the hot water on his muscles, letting out a groan.

His mind wandered to Calliope, to their speed date and drinks, to this morning.

Spike's words replayed in his brain. She's a *muse.*

What was a muse, exactly? Theo wasn't sure what it all entailed, and part of him wanted to talk himself out of believing in Spike's words, but he knew there was a truth in them, even if he couldn't explain it.

Theo ran his hands through his hair, washing it back. The warm water sluiced down his skin, soothing his aching muscles. Falling asleep on Calliope's floor had done a number on his back and shoulders.

His thoughts wandered to last night, to her sweet kiss, and her words that awakened something inside of him.

Worship me.

On your knees.

All yours.

Theo closed his eyes as he fell into the memory, remembering just how Callie *tasted* on his tongue, remembered just how she felt, her tightness wrapped around him. Her mouth on his. Her body pressed against his side as she drifted off to sleep in his arms...

Theo had never felt such intense warmth before. Holding Calliope, worshiping Calliope, it all felt so undeniably right. His cock jumped at the thought and Theo groaned in annoyance.

Now was certainly not the time!

But no matter what Theo did, he could not settle his overactive cock. Not with a cold turn of the faucet or even when he tried to think about *geese* of all things, to alter his thought process. Nothing worked.

Theo groaned, giving into defeat as he wrapped his hand around his cock, relishing in the instant relief it brought.

He closed his eyes, guilt and desire hitting him. And just like before, when he'd tasted her, when he'd felt her, his orgasm started barreling toward him with an irrefutable force.

But in the privacy of his dorm room shower, Theo gave in to his desire, his guilt. He let his cock respond of its own accord, remembering what it felt like for

Calliope to stroke him, touch him. How she'd taken his cock into the back of her throat.

And without warning, Theo's orgasm hit him and he cried out, his voice echoing in the small bathroom. His vision once again turned white, a faint flicker of violet flashing behind his eyes for only a moment.

His entire body loosened, his heart racing as he sprayed the shower wall with his release.

Theo pushed aside his guilt and cleaned himself up, convincing himself perhaps a good masturbation session and a nap would fix him right up. And as he crashed on his bed, he could have sworn he smelled the faintest scent of vanilla and spice.

***

There was a warmth that surrounded Theo he'd never felt before. The world around him was shades of red and violet, melding together with deep shades of green. Up close, the colors blurred, fading into one another.

Theo's gaze traveled down the swooshes and streaks of color, each one standing out against the pale canvas before him. Each one bleeding into the next, he watched streak after streak emerge. But the light flickered, violet and shadow existing together like a lighthouse beacon.

Theodore chased the light, but it seemed too far away. The scent of vanilla was cloying and tempting, and he could hear the sounds around him, or more accurately, a name. His name...

The colors stood out as they became distant, and just as Theodore was about to make sense of what these beautiful colors formed, the sound of the door shutting awakened Theodore from his deep sleep and everything faded into shadow once more.

His vision was blurry once more, but the hangover was gone, thank goodness. He grabbed for his phone, noting it was almost dead, and groaned. Not only was his phone dying, it was nearing four pm. And there had been no word from Spike.

"Theo!" Trick called out. "You back yet, dude?"

Theo groaned once more as he pushed himself up from his bed, heading into the living room slash kitchenette to see Trick looking a little worse for wear.

"He has risen," Trick said with a grin.

"You look like shit. Must've had a good time."

Theo scoffed at him. "Not so bad now. At least my hangover is gone."

Trick made for the refrigerator. "Nice. Must've been epic." The grin on Trick's face was obvious. He wanted details. Details Theo wasn't sure he wanted to give...

"I mean the night wasn't bad, but this morning... could have been better."

Trick sucked in a breath. "Ouch, that sucks, man."

Once again, Theo debated telling his friend the truth. Especially considering he wasn't entirely on board with the truth itself. He couldn't stop thinking about the diviner. Spike said this artifact was one of fate, that it told who someone was supposed to be with. Truth or not, an artifact like that sounded quite powerful, and Theo surmised that if it were to fall into the wrong hands, perhaps it could be disastrous. *If* it was truly a tool of fate, perhaps the thief was trying to influence their own somehow.

But thankfully, Trick was not one to dwell or focus, and instead, he clapped Theo on the back and said, "Glad to hear the Tricky Techniques paid off, man. That's more than I can say for some of us."

Before Theo could ask what exactly his roommate meant, Trick let go of him and headed for the couch, kicking his shoes off and collapsing onto it. Theo noticed the way his shoulders fell, and the deep sigh that escaped him. It was unlike Trick to be anything but confident and cocky, and Theo felt as if at the moment, perhaps he was witnessing a rare sighting. A deflated Trick.

Had something happened to the man? Should he press him about it? Theo knew as much as anyone that most men were not the sharing feeling variety, and Theo wasn't entirely sure he was, either.

Still, there was a part of him that begged to open up, to discuss what had happened. To connect and be there for his friend in the way Trick had for him. But as Theo's gaze drifted to the digital clock on the wall, noting it was nearing four twenty, he felt torn.

He hadn't heard from Spike, and while he knew he could likely text the man, he still felt awkward asking for updates on a situation he wasn't entirely a part of. Yes, he would be working with

Calliope and probably Spike and Isabelle, and yes, there was an emergency—albeit one that his *boss* and co-workers were trying to keep under wraps, which should have been a red flag to Theo—but Theo felt a strange sort of possession when he thought of the— what had Spike called her? A *muse*?

And then Theodore remembered Spike's words, or rather how weighted they'd been.

About how Spike and Izzy would be gone at this time of day, but Calliope would be there. Closing up. Alone.

And Theo surmised that it was probably not safe to be alone in a gallery that had recently been burglarized. So he told himself, he was just being a proactive, good employee. He was just doing what any gentleman would do, and totally *not* stalking Miss Perfect. But the little voice inside Theodore Lange, as quiet as it was, knew the truth he dared not speak.

He was protecting what was *his.*

All yours.

All mine.

So Theo did not press his roommate and instead, left him to his uncharacteristic moment of melancholy and said, "Heading out, I'll be back later."

Trick dismissed him with a grunt and a wave, and Theo headed out the door. The evening sun was warm and it was quite balmy out, but for Theodore it felt as if the sun had truly just come up.

He slid his hands in his pockets, heading for his car. Spike's was much prettier, sleeker than his basic *red*

Focus. Part of Theo was jealous, even though he knew he shouldn't be. He'd worked hard for his car, putting in hours at his uncle's landscaping company all through high school, and it had gotten him from point a to point b for the last few years without protest or issue. But suddenly, Theo felt inadequate, even though he couldn't figure out why.

You know why, he tutted to himself, but instead of dwelling, he picked up his pace and hurried to the parking lot. When he finally found his car amongst the lot, it was nearing four thirty and he sighed.

Turning the car on, the radio blared at him, the familiar sounds of *Undisclosed Desires* filled the air, and Theo couldn't help but chuckle with a dose of sarcasm, since he knew the artist well.

Muse.

How fitting.

It was almost as if *fate* itself was taunting him. If fate existed...

The singer crooned on about wanting to recognize that one's beauty was not just a mask, and Theo felt the words with the utmost truth. So he did not change the channel, and instead turned it up as he pulled out of the parking lot and headed toward the gallery.

CHAPTER SEVEN

CALLIOPE STARED AT the gallery tapes for what felt like the thousandth time. There was not much she and Isabelle had discovered about the theft or the assailant. In fact, after hours upon hours of pouring over footage, there was only two things Calliope *did* know for certain—

The first, was that the assailant who'd stolen the diviner was someone with magical abilities, as they'd blurred the cameras and caused them to malfunction the moment they walked in front of them. Their body did not present as human, and instead, was so bright, it blinded the cameras as they turned to static and black and white, eliminating any chance of identification.

The second thing Calliope knew for certain, was that the magical assailant was a shifter of some sort, only by Spike's admission that the gallery and the display case reeked of a *supernatural* shifter. But Spike, being the hellhound he was, could only ascertain this as a generalized hunch. Typical shifters—wolves, bears, big cats, according to Spike—smelled different than those like him—shifters who were born of a different breed, more rare and in turn, stronger and found more frequently in higher ranking positions. In Spike's case, he had been a shifter in Athena's army, and was kept under the hand of Hades himself, given to Hecate when he'd been injured, where he'd stayed until he found himself human again.

Calliope couldn't help but feel that whoever this mystery assailant was, the fact they were a supernatural shifter did not sit well with her. Because she did not know many supernatural shifters.

Just one.

The thought of calling up Chuck and asking for his help bothered her more than it should have, but she surmised he could possibly be her only option.

Chuck, like Mars, was a power player. He'd cut his teeth in his youth, alongside the God and Goddess of War, as their chariot horse. Athena, Mars, and Pegasus were an unstoppable trio, and at the time, Calliope could not deny the draw there. And Chuck's supernatural form—a stunning white unicorn with large, feathered wings that were as soft as the clouds themselves—held power all on its own, too. His pegacorn dust—the remnants of magic dropped by the creature—was as powerful as the smoke the oracles received their visions from. One only had to be dusted by Pegasus's magical leavings to receive visions of fate and death. A tool Athena and Mars had used to both their advantages at many points in their lives.

And then the band broke up. Athena separated from her father, leaving Mars and Pegasus to their own devices, and thus, Olympus's most prominent bromance was born. Pegasus turned into Chuck, and Chuck became everyone's favorite winged pony. Except hers.

Calliope paused the tape, a soft knocking alerting her. She froze, worry grazing her psyche, but she settled momentarily, thinking perhaps Isabelle or Spike had returned, that they forgot something, or perhaps, Spike had an inkling of what they should be looking for—or who—and she would not *have* to reach out to her ex-lover at all.

But when Calliope reached the door, she felt her blood rush and her heart nearly stop, because it was not Izzy or Spike. It was Theodore.

She blinked, not thinking twice about unlocking the door and pulling it open enough to speak to the man.

"Theo, I did not expect to see you

here until tomorrow."

Honestly, she hadn't expected to see him at all, since what had transpired between them was awkward enough any man in their right mind would have bailed on the situation.

They'd slept together, before knowing the truth, of course, but the truth remained that they'd crossed a line they didn't know existed. And then with the news of the theft, and everything surrounding it, Calliope would not have blamed Theo one bit if he had pulled out of the work-study.

"I thought maybe you could use some company?" he said carefully, that awkwardness and adorable shyness rearing its head once more, making Calliope's insides warm.

She knew she should turn him away.

She did not have time or the emotional bandwidth to deal with romantic entanglements in the midst of everything else, but she could not help herself when Theo was looking at her the way he was.

She opened the door wider, motioning for him to come in.

"I suppose I could give you the tour now, if you like. Before I close up, here."

Theo nodded as he entered, the archway of the door being as thin as it was put him up against her as he walked through.

Calliope tried her hardest to ignore the way her body *heated* when he walked past her, as if her blood itself was on fire.

Bad idea, Callie. Don't go there. You know better.

Still, despite her feelings on the

matter, she couldn't help but close her eyes and breathe in his earthy, spicy scent that warmed her to her toes. And when he'd entered the space, leaving her alone in the doorway once more, she hated the feeling.

She closed the door, locking it and turning to see Theo in the room, his hands slipped into his jean pockets, the motion drawing attention to his broad shoulders and neck, his dark hair.

His perfect, round ass.

Calliope tried to force the thoughts aside. This is certainly not what Theodore Lange came to the gallery for, and she needed to remember where she stood.

She could not become some lust-hungry fool in the midst of such turmoil and unrest. She had a job to do, after all.

"So, typically when we have an exhibition like this, everything remains on display for a few months, but sometimes we display artwork from my classes and the other classes in the art department. And every spring, we do a senior show, where the students get to have their own art show before they graduate, so spring is usually the busiest time here."

Theo nodded as he walked around, checking out the current items on exhibition.

"And what is this exhibition? The one the diviner was part of?"

Calliope casually strolled up to him, as he looked at a vase that once held magical elixirs.

"It was an exhibition on magical

artifacts."

Theo looked at the vase, squinting at it. "Magic, huh? Like, *I put a spell on you*?"

Calliope smirked. "Not quite. The artifacts in this show were believed to have aided the gods themselves. Not as vehicles of power, but rather as artifacts of divination."

"You mean like fortune telling?"

She nodded. "Precisely."

"But, like... don't gods and goddesses divine fate themselves?" he asked as he sauntered to the next item, a scrap of a cloak once worn by the oracle of Delphi.

Calliope looked upon it with fond memory. She'd been quite close with the oracles, then, in her youth.

"Misconception," Calliope said, slowly coming to stand beside Theo once more.

"Gods and goddesses are divine beings, and divine beings can not shift fate for themselves. It would go against the laws of fate."

Theo looked at her with his deep green eyes, twisting his lips. "That kind of sucks. Having all that power and not be able to give yourself what you want?"

His body moved slightly closer to her. She pretended not to notice, though the moment he did so, her insides heated like a flame.

"It is... a nuisance, yes. But... to want is human, is it not?" She licked her lips, staring at Theodore's reflection in the panes of glass surrounding the cloak.

"To err is human," Theo said softly. "Everyone *wants*. Everything wants. The flower wants rain, the dog wants the bone. The kid wants the cookie, and..."

His gaze drifted to hers in the reflection of the mirror.

Calliope noted the way he was looking at her. Like she was the artifact on display, not the scrap of fabric encased in glass. He looked at her as he had last night, right before he'd dropped to his knees. Calliope could not help the way this made her feel, nor could she help the way her body responded of its own accord, leaning closer into his space until their arms were touching. She stared at their reflection as he spoke.

"I want to take you to dinner."

His words were solid, not confident as he had been before, but hopeful. She could feel the truth in them as he spoke, though she could not truly *feel* or sense what it was he wanted, and that made her nervous.

Calliope could always sense what a person wanted, what they needed, especially from her. But it seemed with Theodore next to her and all the insanity of this day, Calliope could not sense anything except the rapid beat of her heart from his words.

"What do *you* want?" he asked carefully.

She closed her eyes, shaking her head as she moved away. "What I want does not matter, Theodore," she murmured as she opened her eyes and headed toward the empty case. The sun was setting and it cast a golden haze through the windows, bathing the gallery in its light.

"Of course it does," he said, coming to stand next to her once more.

Calliope hated the fact his very

presence warmed her, soothed her. But she loved it, too.

To want is a curse all on its own.

"Theodore..." She sighed, just as her stomach growled, protesting her resistance.

He chuckled. "Sounds like you could use some dinner. Have you even eaten at all today?"

She crossed her arms, shaking her head. "That is none of your—"

"I'm just saying you can't survive off pineapple wedges, Callie."

She laughed at his attempt at humor. It was... sweet.

It made her feel warm and cozy, like a fire.

"And what of you, Zorro? Have you taken care of your needs today?"

Theo blushed six shades of red and

Calliope found herself wanting to know *why*. What had she said to irk such a response?

He cleared his throat. "Not all of them."

Her stomach growled again.

Be quiet you!

"You're closing up right?" he asked.

Calliope raised an eyebrow. "I am, but how did you—"

"Spike told me."

Spike. Of course, she'd almost forgotten he'd taken Theo home this morning, forgot they knew each other.

Just another reason why you need to tread lightly, Callie.

"I see."

She stared at the empty case, noting one faint sparkle in the center of the lush blue velvet where the diviner had sat.

Theo looked in the empty case, too. "You still haven't answered me," he said softly.

Calliope stared at the empty space, noticing that once again, Theo was looking at her with that undeniable air of hope.

"You didn't ask me a question, Theodore," she said carefully. "You stated a fact."

He smirked at her. "You going to get all technical on me now, Callie?"

His soft smile was as endearing as it was attractive. Seductive, even.

Callie knew she was waffling. Prolonging the inevitable, but perhaps she liked taunting Theo. More than she wanted to admit to herself, anyway.

"If you want an answer, you have to

ask a question. Or did they not cover that in your college orientation?" she rebuked.

Theo laughed. The sound was just as smooth and warm as it had been before, but this time she could enjoy it fully.

"Ouch," he clutched his chest with his hand. "That hurts."

She shook her head, licking her lips, and let out a giggle of her own.

"Let me take you to dinner," he said, his voice void of the laughter. It was serious, but still carried that air of hope Calliope felt so enticed by.

"Still not a question, Theo," she said with a sigh.

He turned to look at her, and she could not escape the heat of his gaze. She turned to face him.

"You're right, it's not a question," he

said solidly. "I think you *want* to go, but if I ask you, you'll tell me no."

"Theodore..." She groaned, turning away from him once more, her stomach protesting loudly.

"And I don't want you to say no." He walked after her.

"Is that why you came here?" she bit. "To try and get me to go out with you? So you could have a repeat of last night and—"

"No!" he said defensively. "I mean, last night was—"

"A mistake," she said, feeling her throat tighten at the words. All at once, regret flooded her as she heard the sigh escape Theo.

There was a heavy pause, a silence between them, thick with tension until he spoke.

"Then let me make it up to you," he said.

She let out a sigh of her own, turning to look at him once more.

She could see the determination in his eyes, and it reminded her of how he'd been last night. Hopeful, wanting. Wishing.

And she'd guided him into his desire, into his fulfillment, hadn't she?

Something inside of her ached, yearned for Theo's determination. For it was not her *spark* he was asking for.

It was *her.*

Her attention, her permission. Her consent.

"Theo..."

"Just one dinner. I think we've both had a rough day, and if you really feel like what happened between us... was...

a mistake, then let it be my apology."

She twisted her lips as he took two steps closer to her.

"And after tonight, we can start fresh. Forget... forget last night. If that's what you *want*."

Calliope felt conflicted. She wasn't certain what it was she wanted. So, for the moment, she focused on what she *needed*. And Theo was right... she did need to eat.

"Fine," she said matter of factly. "But I am picking the restaurant."

Theo smiled. "Of course. Anything you want, Princess."

The words soothed Callie once more. No four words had ever made her feel so... so...

Theo slid his hands in his pockets. "Promise I'll have you home before bedtime, this time. I mean, it is a school night, right?"

Calliope rolled her eyes as she headed for the office.

"Mhmm. Let me grab my purse first, please."

Theo nodded as she headed for the office, shutting the door briefly. She turned off the tape footage, if only because she felt as if it was truly going nowhere. The only lead she had was that whoever had stolen the a diviner was a supernatural shifter, and she was uncertain what sort of motive one supernatural shifter would have to break into a gallery and steal a diviner. It didn't make sense. The diviner itself had been buried for years, and the only others in existence were in Heaven or Hell. No one used them anymore. Well, no one she knew, anyway, aside from Mars and that had been out of dire circumstance.

Mars…

She stopped for a moment as she thought about the God of War and his recent predicament. His appearance in the presence of the diviner—with Lorelai in tow—had shown him his fate in the midst of losing his power, and as such had shown him the way to redemption.

Could the assailant be in some sort of trouble? Perhaps losing their divine powers?

Chuck may have been an option as far as supernatural shifters went, but Mars was also a valid source of intel. For starters, he was close with Chuck, and may be able to tell her *something* useful in terms of the shifters themselves, perhaps even help her narrow down the *type* of shifter. But Mars had firsthand experience with a loss of power and needing a diviner, so perhaps he could shed some light on the situation as well. And he was a rather *astute* god. His attention to detail was better than most gave him credit for.

And so Calliope rationalized she would call Mars. In the morning, of course. She was rather hungry and did not want to keep Theo or her stomach waiting. So she grabbed her purse and hurried out to find Theo staring at the empty space.

"What color was it?" he asked faintly.

"The diviner? It has no color, truly. Its color appears differently for different... beings."

"What color do most people see?" he

asked. The faintest shimmer of violet strobed across the glass, a trick of the light most likely.

"Humans won't see anything more than a crystal, unless they are divined to be fated to a god or goddess or being of divine nature."

"So, this—" He pointed to the empty space, the specs of debris collected in the velvet.

Calliope moved closer to see what he was pointing at. She got close, looking into the glass. Beneath the light was the faintest collection of dust. Glittering and iridescent. Divine crystals, left in haste, most likely.

"Should be crystal to me, right?" he asked.

Calliope looked up at him in shock. "You see a color?"

Theodore nodded. "Yeah, I do."

His gaze held hers for a moment and she realized how close they actually were.

Her gaze drifted to his mouth. His perfect, pouty lips. Lips she knew just what they felt like against her own, grazing her skin. Bringing her to release.

Her heartbeat quickened and her pulse raced.

The faint rock dust glittered violet and lilac in the light, standing out to her like stars in the night sky, set against the deep blue velvet fabric.

"And what color do you see, Theodore?" she asked, her voice barely a whisper.

"Purple," he said. "Does that... does that mean something?"

It had to be coincidence, and nothing

more. There were no lines or energetic sparks. There was no diviner to truly *divine* a match made by fate. The dust of the diviner left behind was likely just a stain, a remnant of magic, or perhaps even a remnant of the thief's magic who stole it. Perhaps she'd look into that as well in the morning.

She'd have to question Mars about his experience, ask him again what color he saw, perhaps if Lorelai had seen it, too.

"It means that perhaps fate is calling you to its aid," she said softly.

Theo's gaze drifted to her lips and he let out a sigh. "I don't believe in fate. Or magic. Or gods and goddesses from another realm."

The admission saddened her. He did not believe in fate or magic or beings of divinity. He did not believe in her and therefore it was impossible to ascertain that he could believe in *her.*

In a muse.

But belief or not, the diviner had called him. Just as it called everyone it touched. His vision was proof of that.

The spark Calliope felt, the energy boiling between them was proof of that.

Deep down, Calliope knew the truth. She just didn't want to admit it. She feared giving her heart to anyone, least of all a man like Theo.

A non-believer. A young student. Her employee. The reasons were stacking up for Calliope, despite the pull she felt toward him. Her heart beat so loud in her chest she thought he could hear it as he leaned in closer, his lips inches away from hers.

She wanted to kiss him. She wanted to feel his silken lips leading her into that perfect kiss once more. So why could she not bring herself to close the space between them?

His stomach growled and the moment dissipated. It fled into the air as if it had been a figment of her imagination, a trick of the light. Like the diviner dust that shimmered violet, but had diminished as well.

"We should get going," she said, her voice barely a whisper.

"Right." Theo nodded, his voice raspy, tinged with something familiar but yet unfamiliar all the same.

And as he held the door for her, as Calliope locked up the gallery, she couldn't help but feel like something had changed.

Inside her, outside in the world.

She looked through the window of the door, expecting to see the shimmer of the diviner dust catching the low light again, but it was gone.

And so as Theodore led her to his car, as they headed to *La Pear,* Calliope's favorite restaurant, she told herself this would be it. A fresh start, a new leaf. She would leave her moment of passion and perfection with Theodore in the past. She needed to focus on the task at hand—finding the diviner and getting back to her canvas.

***

When they'd arrived at the restaurant, neither of them ordered an alcoholic beverage, as if they both had been thinking the same thing. Instead,

Calliope had opted for a *virgin* piña colada and Theo had opted for a Shirley Temple, complete with five cherries.

"So... not big on French cuisine over here, so what do you suggest?" he asked.

Calliope smiled as she leaned back in her seat. The ambiance and glow of the restaurant added to the small, intimate feel, but it was also open enough and casual enough it didn't feel quite romantic.

Though she was second-guessing herself a bit since she'd never actually been on a date in *La Pear.*

This isn't a date, Callie. It's just a dinner between colleagues. Between friends.

Though, as Callie said the words to herself, they didn't feel right. Theo was certainly a *colleague.* He was a work-study student in her gallery, and therefore, that made him a colleague, but she wasn't sure friend fit the mold, either. One typically didn't sleep with their friends, after all. Lover seemed to fit, but one night of passion did not declare one a lover. One night stand did not fit, and so Callie forced herself to focus on the food and not a defining label for Theodore Lange.

"Do you have any allergies or things you dislike?" she asked.

"Not a fan of mushrooms or tofu, but anything else goes," he said with a smirk. "How about you?"

The way he consistently asked, more and more curious, made her cheeks heat. He seemed to do that frequently. Turn the questions on her.

She didn't hate it, and in fact, a part

of her *liked* his inquisitiveness. It was as if he truly wanted to know *her*.

Most of the men and women Calliope had taken as patrons did not look past the surface. They saw a beautiful muse, a woman of inspiration. They wanted her gifts, her body, her beauty. They wanted her spark, and so they connected through their mutual interest and desire.

But Theodore did not seem to be looking for such things. She could not figure out what it was he wanted from her, and that was as perplexing as it was enticing.

"I have tried many things in my long life, there is not much I dislike."

Theo squinted. "Long life? What are you like… twenty-seven?"

She laughed, unable to help herself.

Of course, why would he think she was anything but what she appeared to be?

And then Calliope realized she was at a crossroads. She could very well dismiss his words, agree with him and he would never be the wiser to who she truly was, *what* she truly was, and they could perhaps truly be *friends.* Colleagues. She could assume the general role she should—teacher, boss, friend.

But Calliope yearned to tell him the *truth,* if only to see how he would react. A man who did not believe in fate and magic may dismiss her admittance as a joke and that would solve the problem, now wouldn't it? His dismissal would solidify the response she needed to forget what had happened between them. It would be easy to separate

Theodore from the mix of men in her life if he truly was someone who didn't *believe* in divinity or magic.

But the spark inside her she felt in Theo's presence did not want to lie. It did not want to hide.

It wanted to be seen, heard, and known in a way Calliope had never known before.

"Technically, I am thirty. By modern beauty standards," she said carefully.

Theo nodded, carefully twisting his lips. "I feel like I'm in the middle of Twilight or something." He laughed.

Calliope furrowed her eyebrows. "What?"

Theo blinked. "You've never seen Twilight? The vampire movie?"

Calliope blinked. "No, I have not."

Theo let out a nervous chuckle. "Well...

there's this scene where, like... Bella, the high school human girl who's in love with Edward, the vampire... she..." He cleared his throat. "God, I can't believe I'm saying this, but... Bella starts to kind of figure out her biology partner is a vampire, and she asks him how old he is and he says 'seventeen.'" Theo deepened his voice, embellishing this vampire character as he explained this movie. "Because, you know, he's a vampire and he's in high school, but people don't know he's a vampire, they just know he's weird and different, and—"

Calliope couldn't help the soft smile that graced her lips as she watched Theodore awkwardly ramble about this movie, his words giving her a newfound sense of adoration and sparking hope anew.

"Well, she asks 'how long have you been seventeen?' and he just kind of ominously says 'a while.'" Theo deepened his voice once more, laughing nervously. "This... kind of feels like that. But if you didn't see the movie, I guess you don't know what I'm talking about."

Calliope licked her lips and shrugged. "Are you asking me how long I've been thirty, Theodore?" Her voice carried an air of teasing, etched with hope and warmth.

He was flirting with her, but it wasn't quite flirting alone. It was more. It was an insinuation. As if the man who claimed he did not believe in fate or magic somehow sensed or believed in her divinity itself.

Theo leaned back in his chair and sipped his Shirley Temple. "Maybe I'm just asking if you're a vampire," he teased.

Callie shook her head. "Fortunately for you, Theodore, I am not."

He set his drink down, his dark green eyes imploring her with intrigue and mischief.

"But I have been thirty for... a little while now. About... one hundred years or so."

He let out a nervous laugh. "Well, I've been twenty-four for a little while, about nine months or so, so I guess that makes us even."

It was the way he said the words, humorously, but also nonchalantly. As if it didn't matter. As if age was truly just a number. Calliope relaxed as she picked up her menu.

"I would suggest the *Duck à l'Orange.*

No mushrooms, and the orange sauce is rather... sweet." She looked up from behind her menu. "And memory serves me correctly, you like sweet things."

Theo smirked at her, just as the waiter came by to take their orders.

"I'll have the *Coq au Vin,* and he will have the *Duck à l'Orange,*" she said with a smile as the waiter took their menus.

"*Merci,*" Theo said with a grin, and Calliope's eyes widened.

The waiter took his leave and Calliope cast Theodore a grin. "I did not know you spoke French."

"I don't. I barely passed high school French. I know three phrases and thank you is one of them."

She shook her head. "What are the other two?"

"*Je ne sais pas,*" he muttered, and

then his cheeks turned scarlet. "*Voulez-vous coucher avec moi, ce soir?*" he said.

Calliope laughed. She truly *laughed.* She seemed to do that a lot with Theodore.

"So all you know is 'thank you, I don't know, and do you want to sleep with me?'" she teased.

"Yeah, and the last one I learned from the song, so I'm not even sure it counts."

Calliope sipped her virgin drink, feeling slightly emboldened. "*Oui,*" she said with a blush of her own.

"Huh?"

"*Oui* means 'yes,' in French. So now you know another word."

Theo smiled. "Up to four words. Before you know it, I'll be able to say a whole phrase." He laughed.

Calliope felt warm and excited.

Talking to Theo even now felt easy. Carefree. His humor, his shyness, his awkwardness... it was endearing. But there was also an understated sort of determination and confidence, buried beneath his surface that she loved seeing. She got the feeling it wasn't something many people were privy to.

"So... did you guys figure anything out? About the missing McGuffin and all?"

Calliope's smile faded.

"Yes and no," she said carefully. She wasn't sure how much she wanted to divulge to Theo. There was still much he didn't know and though he seemed open to some things, he was still a non-believer. She didn't want to ruin the moment and sound like a lunatic. She was having far too much fun enjoying her time with Theo.

"The tapes... were... altered," she said carefully.

Theo sipped his drink, slurping a bit and she had to refrain from giggling.

"Altered how?"

"Well, as I mentioned... the diviner is an artifact of divination for... non-human entities."

Theo nodded. "Right. Gods, goddesses, fairies. Magical beings and stuff."

He didn't sound judgmental. In fact, he sounded intrigued. Analytical almost. Studious.

"Suspend your belief for just a moment, and believe that magic is real," she said softly.

Theo pursed his lips, nodding for her to continue.

"If you believe that, then you would understand that magic can affect everything. Even security cameras."

Theo sat up straighter, leaning in as he regaled her with interest. "Go on."

"The tapes were... altered. Blurred. The thief walked in, blinded the cameras with their light, and blurred the feed. It's impossible to make anything out."

"Could have been a glitch. Internet could have gone down or—"

"No, there was no glitch. It is perfectly timed to their arrival and retrieval. Everything comes back into sharpness the moment they disappear."

Theo rubbed his chin with his thumb and forefinger. "Could have hacked the system."

"Isabelle checked. The system wasn't hacked. It was spelled."

Theo twisted his lips. "So you think whoever stole the Heart of the Ocean, is a... what? A supernatural being? Like a ghost or something?"

Calliope shook her head. "More like a shifter."

Theo's gaze was lost.

Great, now he probably thinks I am a lunatic. Talking of spells and shifters and—

"Like a werewolf?" he asked curiously. "Or a hellhound, or—"

"Yes, like that." She found herself shocked at his notations. Primarily *hellhound.*

Had Spike... told him the truth?

And if so, how much had he divulged?

But before she could press Theo about his sudden interest in the supernatural, the food was delivered and all talk of missing diviners disappeared in favor of dinner.

They both ate without haste, groans of satisfaction echoing between them.

"This is fantastic!" Theo exclaimed with delight, dredging his duck around in the remaining sauce.

Calliope grinned as she finished her bite of chicken. "I had a feeling you would like it."

Theo grinned at her as they continued their dinner, and when the waiter came with the check, Theo did not give any chance for Calliope to intervene, even though she insisted she could indeed, pay for her meal herself.

"I said I was taking you to dinner," he said as he tossed his credit card down and handed the folder to the waiter.

"Theodore…"

"Nope, not going to hear it, Princess."

It was the way he spoke, his humor, his quiet boldness. Calliope liked it far too much.

"Besides, this is my apology, right? I'm the one making it up to you, so…"

The words died in the air as the waiter returned with the folder. Calliope watched as he hurriedly signed and stuck his credit card back in his wallet. Reality struck her that this… this perfect, comfortable dinner was coming to an end. And that meant the night itself was coming to an end, and Calliope did not want it to.

She wanted the night to go on forever, with Theodore.

He rose before she could, so quickly, he moved like a blur. Before she could push her chair out, she felt it drag across the floor and realized Theo was pulling it out. So she could stand.

Gods, he has manners, too. He is certainly too good to be true.

"*Merci,*" she whispered, feeling her cheeks heat.

When she stood, she could see the warmth in his gaze as he looked at her. It appeared he did not want this night to end, either. But end, it had to.

Everything had an ending. Even perfect dates.

It was not a date, Calliope. It was dinner, nothing more.

Though as she followed Theo out of the restaurant into the cool LA night, as she settled into the passenger seat of his car, she felt as if she was trying to convince herself of such things because the reality was so much more frightening than a missing diviner. The sounds of *Maneskin*'s *Begging* filled the space, and Calliope could not help the rapid beat of her heart, nor could she stop herself from stealing glances at Theo. He'd been more than attractive in his dress pants and button down, alongside his mask, but now—in his car, dressed in a simple black shirt and dark jeans, his dark hair smooth and straight, pushed behind his ears, she couldn't help but think he was much more attractive.

Because this... this was the *real* Theo. Simple, understated. A sharp druzy stone embedded in rock.

Beneath the surface, Theo was quite stunning. He turned, catching her glance, and smirked at her. She forced herself to look away. If she did not pay attention, she'd never make it home.

Would that be so terrible?

"Take a turn here," she pointed, alongside the street off campus that led to her apartment.

Theo didn't answer, he just turned down the road, his hands gripping the steering wheel tight. When they'd finally arrived at her complex, he stopped the car, turning it off, but neither of them seemed to want to move.

"Can I walk you to your door?" he asked, his voice barely a whisper.

There was the anxiety she remembered. The uncertainty, and something about that fueled her more than she cared to admit.

"I think I'd like that," she said carefully.

There was a pause before the door

opened and Theo climbed out. He opened her door only a moment later, offering her his hand to help her out. It was a polite gesture, one that felt quite foreign to her. In recent years, and even with David, Calliope's patrons did not expel chivalry. The men she met rarely did things like Theo. Not because they were awful men, but because in today's world, Calliope had noticed a disconnect. Women preferred to do things themselves, as they should, and though many desired men of a certain manner, men did not feel as inclined to put the effort into courting or romancing as they once did, deeming women's independence as emasculation.

But Calliope was certainly capable of opening her own doors, and doing things for herself. She'd become accustomed to it. So much that when Theo went out of his way to be polite and mannerly, she was surprised.

It was not a ploy or thinly veiled manners with ulterior motives. It was genuine.

Theodore *wanted* to be a gentlemen. He *wanted* to be romantic and sweet, because it was who he was.

So, Calliope set her hand in his, and the spark returned. It did not burn as it had before, no. It lit up like static between them.

Thin, lilac fractals danced between their skin for only a fraction of a second before it disappeared.

She glanced up at Theo, and he caught her gaze. His thumb stroked the back of her hand.

"Static electricity," he murmured.

Calliope knew he was trying to convince himself what he'd seen was not real. Looking for some earthly explanation to the spark that existed between them, and at that moment, Calliope realized there was indeed, magic between them.

There was *something* magical and intense and overwhelming between them.

He dropped her hand, and she hated how cold it felt without his palm warming her.

But she did not take his hand as she wanted to. She knew it would only make the ache worse when he left.

So, she walked with Theo by her side, their hands dangling within inches of one another.

And then she felt his fingers graze

hers, almost innocently. He ghosted them along hers, seeking permission.

He *wanted* to hold her hand.

And she wanted him to hold it.

But Calliope could not bring herself to reach for him, and he could not bring himself to steal her hand, and so they walked, grazing, touching ever so faintly with whispers of hope.

When she got to her stoop, she stopped, holding her hands in front of her. She regaled Theo with a steady gaze as the overhead light above her door shone on them.

"Thank you. For your... company, this evening," she said softly.

Theo gave her a graceful smile. "The pleasure was all mine, Callie."

There was pregnant pause as his gaze drifted to her lips.

Calliope's heart lodged in her throat, her insides twisting with anticipation. She leaned in just the slightest, the spark within her catching, remembering just how it felt underneath Theodore's hold, under his kiss.

His voice faltered only slightly when he spoke. "All you have to do is ask," he whispered, leaning in just slightly. The distance between them lessened.

"It's not that simple, Theodore," she murmured, smelling his intoxicating scent. He smelled like cinnamon and cloves and deep, dark forests.

His phthalo gaze caught hers.

"Yes, it is," he insisted, reaching one hand out and tucking her hair behind her ear. The graze of his fingertips on her cheek made her blood rush.

"Perhaps I don't want to *ask* for what

I want anymore. Perhaps I don't want to be told *no*, again."

"Calliope..."

"Perhaps I want someone to *give* me what I want. Without asking. I want someone who *knows* what it is I *need*."

She gazed up at Theo, at his dark, inviting eyes.

Her words made her feel as if she was on the edge of a cliff. One she couldn't escape, one with dark, churning unknown waters below.

And Calliope wasn't ready to jump into its cold, shocking waters.

Theodore leaned in just the slightest, his lips inches away from hers.

She settled her hand on his chest, holding him where he was. As badly as she wanted him to kiss her, she knew if she kissed Theo, he would not leave her doorstep.

Because if Theo kissed her, she would take everything he was willing to give, and she would not let him go.

And she *needed* to let him go. She could not keep him. He was not a thing to possess, but a person. A student.

And it was a school night.

"Good Night, Theodore," she said, her voice darker than it should have been.

He dropped his hand, settling it over her hand on his chest. For a moment there was silence, thick and heavy like an ominous villain.

Theo carefully plucked her hand from his chest and raised her hand to his lips. The spark returned, where he touched her, where his soft lips laid a kiss to the back of her hand.

Violet sparks disappeared into the air

like fireflies.

He kissed the back of her hand softly, before dropping it, his verdant gaze capturing hers once more.

"Good Night, Princess. I'll see you tomorrow."

And with that, Theodore Lange left her on her doorstep, sauntering off to his car.

She watched him leave, unable to tear her gaze from him or the way his perfect ass swayed as he left.

When his car took off, only then could Calliope breathe.

She fumbled with her keys, her hands shaking from the onslaught of emotion and physical response to Theo's sparking touch, to his soft lips. The ache in her heart spread to every inch of her body. Including her pussy.

She grumbled as she shut the door, tossing her keys on the end table. Only a day ago, he'd been here. They'd rushed into her apartment, hands moving of their own possessed accord, mouths seeking one another for more perfect kisses.

She could still remember the feel of his hands on her thighs, of his lips on her skin. Her gaze settled on the room before her, remembering every step, every moment, with new clarity.

One glance at the clock told her it was nearing nine-thirty. It was not late by any means, but Calliope suddenly felt exhausted.

But her fingers twitched, words starting to form in her brain.

Flashes of color begged to be swatched, to make themselves known.

CALLIOPE

Calliope wanted to *paint.*

That itself was a victory, and she felt the tears culminate in her eyes, her chest tightening. She took careful, calculated steps across the living room, remembering every strewn piece of clothing. Every kiss, every touch. Every word uttered.

She remembered his promises.

Anything you want.

She remembered his deep, phthalo green gaze and the red paint smudged along his skin.

When she arrived at her canvas, Calliope stared at the white, bare block in front of her. She grabbed for her palette, fished around across the strewn tubes of paint on the floor, looking for her ultraviolet blue. She grabbed her cadmium red, noting the tube itself was rather full. It had been too long since she used the color, clearly.

She squirted the paint onto her palette, not even bothering to mix it with a palette knife. Her fingers slid through the cool liquid, blurring the colors together. She stood there for what felt like eternity, blending and sliding her fingers through the soft, cool acrylic, watching as it stained her fingers and hand. And when she'd gotten several varying shades of purple—from plum to lilac and in between, she took her fingers and touched them to the canvas.

One streak of violet paint stained the surface, bleeding into the taut fabric and it felt like a weight had been lifted from her shoulders.

Calliope closed her eyes, letting the tears come as she followed her inner muse, the inspiration taking hold. Her fingers glided across the canvas over and over until she opened her eyes to see the shape of a star.

A spark.

Shimmers of violet and mauve and purple and blue that hadn't mixed well, streaks of red that refused to be diluted in anything.

Relief flooded her.

She'd done it; she'd broken her block.

Calliope grinned as she sauntered to her bathroom, removing her clothes if only so she could bathe and ready herself for bed. And as she crawled into bed, she breathed in deep, the faint scent of Theodore's cologne clinging to the air. To her pillow.

She closed her eyes, breathing in deep, the scent igniting her inner spark.

Warmth flooded her, her memories once again circling her like prey.

His mouth, his tongue, his laugh, his eyes...

Theo filled Calliope's psyche, and she was too tired to fight. So she let herself wander down the memory of his kiss, his touch, his smooth voice. She let herself remember just how he could please her.

And the thought of his devotional tongue sparked desire in her loins once more.

She knew she should *not* pursue such fantasies. She'd promised herself tonight would be a fresh start, that she could put aside what had happened and start the semester anew.

But Calliope knew as she let her hand travel underneath her nightgown, as her fingers slid between the fabric of her already soaked panties, that there was no forgetting Theodore Lange.

Because fate had brought him to her, that she was sure of. And Calliope had a feeling if they somehow found the diviner, it would divine the truth in its stone, the same way it longed to divine through its dust.

Theodore could not see the color of the diviner unless he was divined for someone.

Perhaps *her*.

It was wishful thinking, Calliope knew that. For she'd only seen the color of the diviner on her own, not with another person. Even when she'd lain her gaze upon it, when Mars and Athena and Isabelle and Spike and Lorelai had been there, she hadn't seen a line toward... well, anyone. All she'd seen was the thin violet line, shooting out, but without an end. It was short, perhaps because she had no divined mate. Perhaps, the diviner was only showing her her openness to be a muse, to be open to so many.

But now, perhaps, Calliope thought, it was because Theo was simply not in her proximity yet.

Her fingers slid inside her entrance as she tried to push the thought aside. She could not afford to fall for such fantasies.

But the fantasy of Theo wanting her, of him *giving* her what she wanted more than anything else—to be *his* in all senses of the word—was too much to fight.

And so Calliope gave herself to her fantasy, telling herself it was just for tonight. Tomorrow, things would be different.

Tomorrow she would call Mars and inquire about his knowledge of supernatural shifters, of his experience with the diviner, and she would find a way to bring the diviner back, and when she did bring it back, she'd know for certain if she was right about Theo.

Until then, she vowed she would keep her distance from him. She had to. Because if Theo was *not* the mate she wished him to be, it would be too painful to bear, if she was too entangled.

She closed her eyes and chased the memory of his lips on her clit, his fingers pumping inside her. She tried her best to mimic his movement, but it was no use. It wasn't the same and it would never be the same.

She thrust her hips against her hand, inserting another finger inside herself as she flicked her clit with her thumb. She lost herself in the motions, the feelings. The memory.

All yours.

Her orgasm built, steady and slow as she wandered down the paths of her psyche, of last night. And when she remembered that feeling of wholeness, of being lost and found all at once while he filled her, she came with a moan full of relief and exhaustion hit once more. Calliope removed her hand from her slick channel, her pussy spasming like sparks beckoning to catch onto kindling.

It wasn't enough, but it would have to do. Because Calliope could not have what she wanted, but in her dreams, she found herself entangled in shades of violet and green, once more.

CHAPTER EIGHT

THEO SIGHED AS anxiety built within him. He was still rather tired, being as he hadn't slept particularly well the previous night. He'd woken up hard, twice, after dreaming of Calliope, which was bad enough, but staying quiet it seemed was not as easy as it used to be. For when Theo thought of Calliope, stifling his moans was the equivalent of shutting up a magpie.

He'd came, both times, nearly

suffocating himself in his pillow so as not to wake Trick. His roommate might have been accepting of many things, but he wasn't certain he'd be so cool with being woken up in the middle of the night because Theo couldn't keep his cock settled.

Which was... new.

Up until recently, Theo had barely engaged in any sort of self-pleasure. He masturbated frequently enough, once or twice a week just to make sure everything still worked, and to let off stress before a large test or whatnot, but it was as if ever since he'd been with Calliope, his cock had woken up with renewed life.

And with it being quite a sensitive member to begin with, Theo wasn't sure this was a good thing. He worried he'd end up one of those individuals who couldn't put their cock down, or worse, go blind from all the self-pleasure.

"Hey, Theo!" A feminine voice pulled him from his thoughts, and he looked up to see Isabelle and Spike waving at him. But they were not alone. A tall, slender woman with vibrant red hair, and an older, rougher looking man with dark hair and a faint beard were also with them.

"Hey," he said, as Isabelle shoved him in front of the redhead and the grizzly looking man.

"This is Theo, I was telling you about him yesterday. He's the new gallery work study. Theo, this is Lora. She works at the gallery with us, too."

Lora held out her hand to shake his, and he took it politely.

"Oh, hey, nice to meet you."

I guess it makes sense the other work studies are probably art majors.

He looked at Spike, who seemed to be sniffing the air and making a face.

It dawned on Theo that Spike had mentioned being a *hellhound*, capable of smelling things apparently humans could not. The jury was still out on whether or not Theo believed him, but the action would make sense.

And suddenly, Theo wondered if he'd remembered to put deodorant or cologne on this morning.

"This is Mars," Lora said with beaming eyes. "I finally talked him into taking an actual class!"

Mars nodded at Theo.

"Take it you aren't an art major?" Theo chided.

Mars shook his head. "Lorelai said a good mate is *supportive.*"

It was not the way he said the words, but rather the words themselves. Or rather, *one* word.

Mate.

Something about that word echoed in Theo's brain, familiar yet foreign at the same time. The word drummed up memories of Calliope, or rather the moment he'd found himself buried inside Calliope until he couldn't think straight.

He'd called her his, but there was a desire that *yours* wasn't the right word. Mate felt like the right word, but Calliope certainly wasn't his *mate.*

He wasn't sure what she was, entirely. One night stand wasn't correct, and girlfriend was far too stage five clinger even for him, but *mate...*

It made him feel warm, content. At peace.

I need to get to bed early tonight. Clearly sleep deprivation is affecting me.

Theo pulled on his bookbag as he nodded at Mars. "I see."

"You didn't mention you were taking one of Callie's classes," Spike said as Izzy patted the desk next to her.

"Oh, you know Callie?" Mars asked curiously.

Theo cleared his throat as the reality of the words hit him. Callie's *class.*

Callie is... a teacher, too? Panic hit him.

Did I sleep with my fucking teacher? The realization, worry, and lust hit him all at once as Izzy patted the chair once more.

"Yeah, he's her new muse or

whatever," Isabelle said nonchalantly.

"What?" Theo's voice cracked.

"Here, you're going to want a front row seat. You get so many more details that way."

Theo's blood chilled. "I'm sorry, did you say *Callie* teaches this class?"

"Yeah. Lifestyle Drawing is one of Callie's classes..." Spike said as if the information was common knowledge. "I thought you knew that, because usually the work study requires at least one art class to apply."

Theo blinked. It was true; he did know that. He'd signed up for his art electives because he needed them for his graduating credits, but also, he'd done it to ensure he wouldn't be rejected for the work study.

He'd looked at the schedule,

numerous times, but he hadn't connected the instructor's name to—

"Good morning, class," Calliope's sweet, chime-like voice rang out and Theo turned slowly to see Calliope, coming through the door with a coffee in her hand, dressed in a form-fitting black and grey tweed skirt with a matching black blouse that drew attention to her ample round breasts.

Theo's cock noticed the way her nipples peaked through the fabric, twitching in response.

Oh, fuck.

Calliope's gaze settled on him as she froze in the middle of the room.

Theo felt like he might pass out.

Especially because she looked quite appetizing in her matching outfit, her heels making her lithe legs stand out, her dark hair spilling over her shoulder. Breasts pushed together to give ample cleavage.

"Theodore... I didn't expect to see you this *morning*."

Izzy nudged him in the ribs. "This is the part where you say good morning, idiot."

Isabelle's words pulled him out of his stupor and he cleared his throat. "Uh huh. Good morning, Callie."

She looked from him to Mars, moving past him without any other acknowledgment. Like once again, he was beneath her somehow. Like she needed to *get away*.

"Boy, am I glad to see you," she said with a sigh. The words cut Theo deeper than he knew they should have.

Who is this guy? What does Callie

want with him?

"Don't get excited, I'm just here because Lora—"

"I need to talk to you after class, not here." Calliope looked at them all as students continued to pour in and take their seats.

"All of you."

Her gaze settled on Theo and for a moment he felt as if time itself stopped.

She offered him a faint smile before taking her spot at the front of the room.

"You think it's about the diviner?" Isabelle asked.

"What about the diviner?" Mars asked.

Lorelai took her seat next to Mars, while Spike took the center.

Izzy sat next to Theo.

"It was stolen," Izzy said in hushed

tones.

"Stolen?" Mars's voice elevated as Spike shushed him.

"Yes, keep your voice down!"

Theo nodded at Spike. "Callie said you think a shifter stole it, right?"

Mars looked down the line at him, but it was Lorelai that spoke, pulling his attention.

"A *supernatural* shifter," Spike noted. "Like me."

"Wait, does he know—" Lorelai pressed as Izzy waved her off.

"Yeah, Spike told him all the tea yesterday."

"I'm not sure I believe in all this shifter fate magical rock stuff but—"

They all raised their eyebrows at him.

"What?"

"You don't believe in magic and you're

dating a literal muse?" Izzy bit.

"Dating? It was Theo's turn to raise his eyebrows.

Not that he didn't *want* to date Calliope, but he knew one night of sex and one romantic dinner did not equal a relationship. Especially not a date that ended without a kiss.

Well, to be fair I did kiss her. Just not like I wanted to...

At that moment, Calliope's gaze caught his as Spike said, "Let's not get carried away. No one said they're dating."

Isabelle huffed in annoyance. "Yeah, okay, and I'm not a monster fucker."

"Izzy!" Spike's voice hitched an octave and his cheeks reddened like tomatoes.

Mars eyed Theo suspiciously.

"Okay, class, please find your seats

and we'll get started with introductions!" Callie called out and Theo forced himself to look away, though he could feel Mars's eyes on him a mile away.

What is his problem?

Thankfully, once class started, Theo was able to focus on the task at hand. The class. After Calliope had given her professor's introduction and everyone had done their round table introductions, it was time for drawing.

Theo had expected a nude model, but it turned out, the only model was a clothed volunteer.

Lorelai.

Calliope positioned Lorelai on a chair, set some vases of fake flowers around her, and draped a long, pale pink fabric over that looked like cut shears.

It wasn't *Girl With A Peal Earring* but

Theo wasn't sure what he expected. He held his charcoal stick in his hand, trying to figure out how to start, when Spike leaned over to his desk.

"Don't overthink it. Just draw a line and go from there."

Theo looked at the dark-haired, dark-eyed man beside him.

"Guess you've done this before?"

Spike nodded. "Last semester, I took Callie's painting class. She's not worried about if your stuff is perfect, she just wants you to *feel* it, you know?"

Theo chewed on Spike's words. Painting class?

"She teaches painting, too?"

Spike nodded. "Drawing, Painting, and Ceramics."

Theo nodded, letting his hand draw a line on the paper in front of him. It was just a black line. Nothing special. Hardly anything to get excited over. He looked at Lorelai, trying to find a place to start again.

"I have painting 101 this semester, too," Theo mused as he focused on Lorelai's arm.

Spike chuckled. "Did you pick these *before* or after your speed date?"

"Before."

Spike grinned. "And you don't believe in fate?"

Theo shrugged, going back over the line. "I don't know, honestly. It sounds nice, but... in my life, I haven't really seen fate working in my favor."

Spike drew a line on his paper, and it was much more fluid than Theo's straight one.

"I don't know, I think fate's all about

perspective. The literal Fates... they work in puzzles and riddles. They don't like things simple, so sometimes it seems like it's against you, but... in the end, it all leads you to the same place."

Theo watched Calliope as she started to circle the room, stopping at each student's desk.

"If everything is already divined, though, then nothing is left to chance. Everything's just a game."

Spike swooshed a large arch, filling in some space.

"Not true. Fate and free will are different. I was meant to find Izzy, but the choices I made, the things I did—" Spike let out a heavy sigh. "Before I got there, that was my choice. I would've always found her, but... maybe it wouldn't have been the right time otherwise."

Theo watched as Calliope stopped, smiling at a student. She illustrated something with her hands, pointing.

The light in her eyes was beautiful, but then again, so was she.

What had they called her, a... muse?

"I don't know. I like to think we can choose our own fate, you know?"

Spike smirked. "Or maybe your fate is to discover it."

Calliope moved steadily along the desks, and Theo tried his best to focus on the model, on getting out some shapes. His doodles had not prepared him for this.

Though, soon, Theo discovered that there was a sort of rhythm to the lines and shapes as he repeated them. He took his time, trying his best to capture what he was looking at, but there seemed to be a disconnect between what he saw with his eyes and what he felt with his heart.

He felt her before he saw her. Felt that undeniable buzzing of electrified energy that always seemed to exist when she was near.

Was it fate? Magic? Theo didn't know. But whatever it was, it was real.

Very real.

"I did not think you an artist, Theo," she said carefully. Platonically. *Professionally.*

Theo knew on some level, Calliope was being professional as not to draw attention or show favoritism, and it was the logical thing for her to do. They were both adults. Consenting adults. But Theo garnered perhaps some distance was not a bad idea. Until he could truly figure out where he stood with Miss Perfect.

"I mean... you don't have to be an artist to appreciate art, right?" he asked with a half smile, hoping it would detract from the mess of lines and shapes on his paper. For Theo had the strangest *need* for validation, wanting Calliope's praise.

He remembered how good it felt the last time he had heard it, how he had felt like the world was at his feet from just those two words. *Good Boy.*

Spike chuckled beside him.

"This is true," Calliope said. "But if appreciation is your goal, I am not sure a lifestyle drawing class will make you appreciate the craft. Drawing is rather... whimsical. It is meant to be felt, not seen."

Theo shifted in his seat, the motion putting him next to her a fraction. Their arms barely touched.

"But you have to *see it*, too. You have to look, study, record what you see. To understand it, to know what it feels like."

Calliope's amber eyes glistened as she looked at his paper. "This is true. But what you see may differ from what Spike does. Or what I see. So how do you convey your message if your audience varies? You have to appeal to their sense of heart. Their emotion."

She ran her hand down one of his lines. "You can tell a lot about a person by the fluidity in which they draw. Precision is what most strive for. They think lines need to be straight—" She carefully traced Lorelai's arm. "—that precision and accuracy are the makers of true art."

She pressed her fingers into his charcoal, wiping it, smudging it. Breaking his beautiful line. "But true art comes from the unexpected. The mistakes that create new paths of exploration."

Theo's gaze drifted as she plucked her fingers off the page.

"Do not limit yourself, Theo. Try to see the lines and shapes as choices, not art itself. Look for the imperfections and you will appreciate perfection."

He caught her gaze for a moment. A minuscule moment. But however small it was, that moment for Theo was infinite. It was perfectly imperfect.

She smiled as she moved to Spike, and Theo looked back at his canvas with a renewed sense of confidence and dare he say... inspiration.

He flipped his paper, instead of focusing on Lorelai, he noted the *perfect shape* of Calliope's side profile. How her dark hair fell over her shoulders. How her lips parted as she spoke. And so, Theo looked closely, recalling his own memories, of what he deemed perfect. And that was what he drew. Her slender neck, her silky hair. Her long eyelashes. There were no flaws in Calliope's design.

Not a one.

When it was time to pack up, he realized he'd gotten lost in her details.

"Not bad," Lorelai's said with a smirk.

"Thanks," Theo said, his cheeks heating as he flipped the paper. "Guess I was just feeling a little inspired."

Spike chuckled as the class thinned

out and Calliope called them over.

After a brief recant of the situation, Mars agreed to discuss his apparent own divine experience with Calliope, while Isabelle and Lorelai took off for their next class.

"You ready for your first day, Picasso?" Spike joked.

He shrugged. "No time like the present."

He caught Calliope's stare, and the moment he did, she blushed, turning away.

"I'll be by later to close," she said, but she looked at *him* when she said the words.

Theo couldn't help but grin. "Sounds good."

And with that, he followed Spike to the gallery, feeling inspired by more than just his artistic accomplishments.

CHAPTER NINE

MARS RAISED AN eyebrow at Calliope as he leaned his large arms across her demo desk.

"So... you're courting patrons again, I see?"

Calliope did not meet his gaze. "Theodore is *not* a patron."

That much was true, but Calliope was still out on what exactly Theo was. He was her student. Her employee of sorts. And perhaps, he was even a man she met in a bar. Those lines were definitive. Simple to understand.

But she also knew he was so much more than that. He was sweet, perhaps even naive, at times, because he was *twenty-four,* but he was also bold and confident and handsome and endearing and he was a rather good kisser.

But most of all, he was *inspiring.*

"He is a... friend." Calliope did not like the word. It didn't feel right, but she also knew calling Theo anything more than such right now would have been presumptuous. One night of sex and one date-not-date did not equal a relationship.

Was that what Calliope wanted? A relationship? With Theo?

She wasn't sure the answer was no, but saying yes felt monumental in a way she wasn't entirely ready for. Saying yes felt like an earthquake. For Calliope had not been in a *relationship* since she and Chuck had been young. And it had not ended well. It was then she decided to keep her affairs short and sweet, on all accounts. Falling in love was not in the cards for Calliope, and perhaps the separation, the solid line she drew between her patrons and herself was more about protecting her peace and her heart than it was about anything else. It was simple. Rules defined to keep everyone safe. Her patrons would never *love* her. They only loved and desired what she could give them, her spark. And when the well would run dry and the spark died, they'd be on their merry way. David Green was proof of that.

And for a long time, that had been

fine with Calliope. She'd accepted it was her destiny, her fate. That was, until she met David and fell for his charms, his saccharine words and spellbinding promises.

And then he'd simply broken all of that, thrown away his inspirational sonnets and words when the well ran dry.

And the void thrived in the emptiness until it had consumed all that was and all that would be for David Green, leaving Calliope to tend to the ashes left behind in his wake.

"Mhmm... well, I'm sure you know that boy does not see you as a friend," Mars said with a smirk.

"I do not wish to discuss my love life, or lack thereof, with *you,* of all people, Mars." Calliope huffed as she tidied her brushes in their jar.

He snickered. "Ah, I have struck a nerve, I see."

She rolled her eyes at him and he held his hands in the air in mock defense.

"What *did* you want to talk to me about that you couldn't say in front of your little disciples?" he asked, his voice still tinged with humor.

Calliope twisted her lips, regaling him with her gaze. "The diviner was stolen, as you know."

Mars nodded. "What does that have to with me? Why is that my problem?"

Calliope crossed her arms. "Spike said he *scented* an animal. A shifter."

"And that matters to me because..."

"Because, Mars, the shifter Spike is claiming to scent, is not your run of the mill wolf or big cat. He claims it's a supernatural shifter."

Mars raised an eyebrow. "Like a hellhound? One of Hades's?"

Calliope shifted her weight. "Hades no longer controls the hellhounds. He's mortal, remember?"

Mars shrugged. "Cate ain't mortal. Last I checked, Hades literally *gave* her a hellhound, so—"

"Yes, and that hellhound is walking around on two legs, mated to a vampire for the rest of eternity. And you yourself know hellhound shifters are extremely rare." She chewed on her lip, not wanting to speak her thoughts, but knowing if she did not get them off her chest, they would eat her alive. And that was why she'd called Mars to her desk, after all. She'd spoken with Spike and

Theo, and Isabelle and Lorelai had promised to be on the lookout as well.

But Mars... Mars was of a different caliber, and he was also close to her suspect. Calliope couldn't prove anything, but she felt an aching in her gut. She knew it didn't make sense, but she could not refute it nonetheless.

"Have you heard from Chuck recently?" she spoke carefully.

Mars did not miss her insinuation, his eyebrows furrowing. "So that's why you wanted to speak to me," he nipped. "You think *he* has something to do with the disappearing diviner?"

Calliope did not miss the tone of Mars's voice, and she immediately regretted her words. *So much for tact, Callie.*

"I am not ruling it out, Mars, and

neither should you."

Mars crossed his arms. "What reason would Chuck even have to *steal* a diviner? The guy is swimming in pussy."

Calliope felt defensive. "I don't know! That's why I'm asking *you*, Mars. You are the only one I know closest to him. You would know better than I—"

"Yeah, we *were* close. Thick as thieves, but—"

Calliope did not miss his sarcasm, but she noticed there was also an air of hurt in his words. Hurt, in Mars's voice was...

Uncharacteristic. Odd.

"But what?"

Mars shook his head. "Sometimes people change, you know. And some people... some people don't. Some people can't embrace change."

Calliope noted the sadness in his voice. "Did you two have an argument or something?"

Mars shook his head once more. "No, it wasn't like that, it was just..." He let out a heavy sigh. "He's my best friend, Callie. You know that. Nothing's ever going to change that, but he felt like..."

Calliope suddenly realized the problem as Mars answered his buzzing phone, smiling when he looked at it.

"It's Lorelai, hold on," he said as he tapped out a text.

Pegasus had lost his wingman. He'd lost his partner in crime. To a human. A human who had saved his life.

The puzzle pieces started to fall into place, but was Chuck—was *Pegasus,* the god shifter she once knew—would he do something like this?

A god as powerful as him certainly didn't need to resort to *stealing*. And as much of a pain in the ass as the man was, how cocky and conniving he could be, Calliope had never known him to steal anything but hearts and beds.

"You could just ask him, you know. You don't have to converse through *me*."

Calliope pursed her lips. "And you think he'd tell me the truth?"

Mars shrugged. "You know him pretty well, too. I don't know what you're so afraid of, why you two won't speak."

Calliope let out a heavy breath. "It's not that simple, Mars."

"You always say that, Callie. You act like things are so complicated, but they aren't. Chuck's not the same guy you once knew. He's changed."

Calliope knew Mars was right, the

winged pegacorn *had* changed. Perhaps he had fallen as Mars once had…

"When is the last time you saw him?" she pressed.

"Personally? A couple months. But I know he still hangs out at the *Den of Sin* pretty frequently. If you… wanted to, you know, stop by for a chat with the guy."

Calliope looked away, shaking her head. "I'm not sure that's such a good idea."

She looked at the clock, realizing her next class would be starting soon.

"Just… think about it, okay?" Mars said carefully.

Calliope nodded. "I will think about it, but perhaps you should also remember that you *owe* me still. A favor."

Mars's gaze narrowed. "You cashing in your chip already, Cal? Shit, you really have something against the guy."

It wasn't that Calliope hated her ex-pegacorn beau. It was more or less, he aggravated the hell out of her. Chuck was not practical. He lived life on the edge, and he lived with no consequences. It did not matter to him who he fucked, where he landed, or where he went. Life was his buffet and a long time ago that had been attractive, but it had gotten stale. The inspiration dried up, as all sparks did, and when the sun came out, she had realized that she could not live on the edge of a cloud. Calliope longed for *more.*

She longed for love and devotion, two things the god shifter was not capable of. For Pegasus needed to be adored and praised, to have his coat stroked and then some. And in Pegasus's life, there was only room for one beautiful creature. Himself.

"My class is starting in ten minutes," she said pointedly.

Mars hummed in response. "Okay, I see. I'll catch you later, Cal. Let you know if I hear anything, okay?"

She nodded, and with that, Mars left her alone in the studio.

***

When her classes were finally done for the day, Calliope relished in the relief. Her stomach growled and she fought with the decision to stop and eat or to head directly to the gallery. She'd damn near lost her appetite at the thought of speaking to her ex, not because she was afraid, but because she just didn't want to unearth her own dirty laundry in the process. What was in the past was in the past.

And that was where it needed to stay.

She'd finally settled on a sandwich wrap from the cafe on campus and a coffee, which she practically inhaled on her way to the gallery. It was nearing five when she arrived, and though she expected to see Theodore and Spike, she did not expect to see Isabelle, Lorelai, *and* Mars. She blinked, her gaze settling on the group who were hunched in a huddle on the floor. Calliope could feel the tension in the air and then she noticed the broken case.

The case the diviner had been in was shattered, the exposed velvet catching the light. She did not think, she just acted. Locking the door, she sprinted over to their huddle to see they were all hovering over one person in particular.

Theodore.

"Oh Gods, is everything all right?" Calliope asked as she pushed through Spike and Mars.

Theodore rubbed his eyes as Isabelle helped him sit up.

"How many fingers am I holding up?" Mars asked, as Spike and Theo turned to face her.

"I'm fine," Theo mumbled, his voice annoyed. "Seriously, I just tripped over my own fucking feet, I—"

"No, you are not fine," Lorelai said matter of factly. "You hit your head, you could have a concussion..."

"He doesn't have a concussion," Isabelle tutted. "Like *one* piece of glass hit him. He's fine."

"See, the vampire says I'm fine..."

Theo murmured.

Isabelle chuckled. "Thought you didn't believe in magic and vampires and all that jazz—"

Theo groaned. "Maybe that glass did hit me harder than I realized."

Calliope reached out, setting her hand on his arm, and he looked up at her.

"Callie, I—"

"What happened?" she asked as she knelt on the floor beside him.

Spike scooted over to make room for her, not saying a word. Mars did the same.

"I don't know, I was just... you know that debris left behind? The purple dust or rocks or whatever—"

Everyone turned to look at her with interest. Mars especially.

"Yes," she said shakily.

"Well, I kept hearing this whistling sound and it sounded like it was coming from the display so… I just got up to check it out and saw the rock dust or whatever was like… moving. Like jumping around and—"

"Theodore went to remove the case and the whole thing just shattered," Spike said in alarm.

"It literally just happened, Cal," Mars said carefully.

"Right, of course. Are you sure you are all right, Theo?" She reached out, trailing her fingers over his temple. He didn't *look* hurt. There were no scars or wounds or even a pink bump.

His verdant gaze drifted to hers and his cheeks pinkened as he said, "I am now," and Calliope felt her heart beat faster.

Mars chuckled beside her.

Calliope blushed as she dropped her hand.

"Alright then, get up. Don't just sit there," she nodded to Mars and Spike.

"We've got a shattered case to clean up and I'd like to speak to Theodore. Alone."

Lorelai and Izzy nodded as Spike touted, "I'll get the broom."

Calliope helped Theo up as Mars brushed past her, heading to Lorelai. Calliope guided Theo to the lounge couch in front of the large painting from the exhibit. One she did not care for. A large painting of several muses dancing around a fire with a satyr, a centaur, and... a pegacorn.

It was like Chuck was everywhere,

when he was nowhere. A constant reminder of youthful innocence and soured friendship.

"What really happened, Theo?" she asked as she guided him to sit down. She sat beside him, the cushions shifting from her weight, sliding her closer to him.

He sighed, looking back at her. "I just... heard the sound and it was driving me crazy, so I went to check it out, and just... poof. I saw the shimmer of violet and I went to open the case so I could see what was going on and it just shattered to pieces. I'm sorry, I—"

"No, no. Don't be sorry, it's not your fault. Perhaps it was just too hot or the sun hit the dust wrong, or—"

"Or maybe I'm just cursed," Theo said with a smirk. "Maybe fate changed its mind about me."

Calliope shifted beside him, holding his gaze. His dark eyes were soft, glistening with that spark of hope but also sadness, as if Theo truly believed he was not *good enough* to be chosen by fate.

How wrong he was.

He ran his hand along his face, and she noticed as he did so, the sparkle of dust along his cheek. Iridescent dust.

The diviner itself did not leave glittery dust in its wake, and the debris left on the velvet, the glittering debris was not iridescent in nature.

Calliope grasped his hand and turned his palm over. His hand was *covered* in iridescent dust, shimmering like diamonds in the low light.

"Whoa... what the hell is that?"

Theodore asked.

Calliope's blood chilled.

"Is this the hand you touched the display with?" she asked.

Theo nodded, shifting his position. The motion drew them closer together, until their thighs were touching. Neither made it a point to move.

"Yeah, why..."

Calliope's fingers slid over his palm, through the familiar silica-like dust. There was only one creature she knew who could leave such a bright, illuminating film in his wake.

A creature who was looking more and more guilty by the minute.

"It's pegacorn dust," she said carefully. She traced her finger along his palm lines. "Left by a pegacorn when they transform."

"A pegacorn? What the fuck is that?" Theo asked in alarm.

Everyone turned their way.

Mars's heavy gaze met hers.

"A pegacorn is a fabled creature. A unicorn with wings. Extremely rare," Mars said.

Theo looked between them all. "How rare?"

Mars licked his lips. "As in, only one exists."

Theo looked up at Calliope.

Her heart ached, her stomach churning. But Calliope did not look at Theodore. She stared at Mars, imploring him with her gaze.

"Guessing you two know a pegacorn," Izzy asked.

Lorelai interjected, her gaze dancing between Mars and Calliope. "You don't think—"

Mars sighed. "I don't know what to think anymore."

Calliope felt a tight squeeze upon her hand, the motion jolting her from her dissociation. She turned to see Theo holding her hand.

His thumb brushed the back of her hand, spreading sparkles of pegacorn dust along her pale skin.

"This... this is a good thing, right?" Theo asked. "I mean, if there's only one pegacorn and his prints are all over the glass... then... it's pretty clear who's the thief, right?"

Calliope gazed down at him. Her heart felt torn between admitting the truth and withholding it.

"That doesn't explain why the glass shattered, though," Izzy chimed in.

"Izzy's right. Pegacorn dust isn't volatile. It doesn't usually react to humans."

Mars met her gaze. "What was the sound like?" he asked.

Theo squeezed Calliope's hand, settling it in his lap.

She didn't let go, for fear if she did, she may disappear completely. Everything was converging on her at once.

"What do you mean?" Theo asked.

"I mean, was it like a whistle or a song, or like a strung guitar string—"

"Yes," Theo's eyebrows shot up. "The last one... like a long note. It was... driving me crazy."

"Someone care to explain?" Lorelai pressed.

"The diviner shows you your fate,

your mate for eternity," Mars said.

Calliope shrank in the seats, curling closer to Theo, who did not push her away. For she knew what Mars was going to say and she wasn't certain she was ready to hear it.

She wanted to crawl into a ball, disappear, and never return.

"And in most cases, both parties will see the thread. Fate's thread. It will lead them to their mate."

Spike nodded. "Right. Theo said he saw a violet thread, and Calliope did, too, so why—"

Mars gave her a soft, understanding look. It was odd to see such a look on the God of War's face.

"Because there's another thread, entangled with Calliope," he said. "And Theodore here—her *mate*—" He spoke the word aloud and the room fell silent.

Theo looked up at Mars, his eyebrows furrowed. "Mate?"

Mars sighed and Calliope closed her eyes. Theo's hand grew warm against hers.

"Yes, Theo. I believe you and Calliope are destined to be together. But—"

"But what?"

Calliope felt the tears sting her eyes. She could not hide the truth any longer. No matter how badly she wanted to.

"I'm fairly certain your thread reacted to *his*. The one who is entangled."

"The pegacorn guy?" Theo asked faintly. He turned to Calliope and in his gaze she could see the anxiety, the fear. The panic.

In her experience, men did not respond well to the idea of being bound eternally. Human or god.

"Callie, look at me..." he implored.

She hated how she did so without a second thought. No human should be able to pull her attention, her command, quite like this.

She'd barely known Theodore for three days.

Three days, and it was as if he'd wedged his way into her heart, yet always been there. It was as mysterious as a masquerade, as powerful as a chariot in the sky.

She looked at Theo with watery eyes, choking back a sob. His green gaze captured hers.

"It's true," she said. "I didn't want to tell you, I know you don't believe in fate or destiny, or—"

"I might not believe in those things,

Calliope, but I don't *have* to believe in them, to believe *you.*"

His words settled in the air between them. Calliope nodded.

"And this pegacorn, you're sure he has the diviner?" Lorelai asked.

Mars nodded.

"It makes sense," Spike said. "Pegacorns wield light magic. Which the tapes were blinded by a bright light. And Theo's thread lit up, reacted to the pegacorn dust. Broke the glass. So... I'd say all roads point to pegacorn."

"But how do we... untangle Callie and this winged asshole?" Izzy asked.

Mars crossed his arms, twisting his lips. "Well, for starters, we have to get the diviner and then use it to sever the bond between Callie and Chuck."

Hearing the words out loud were too

much. Calliope felt the tears, the ache in her chest erupting like a volcano.

Theo pulled her into his arms, and she let him, forgetting for a moment they had an audience.

"Hey, it's okay, don't worry, Princess, we'll figure this out," he whispered in her ear.

She wrapped her arms around him, the spark in her catching once more as his words settled on her.

His arms were warm, his touch soft. She could hear the steady beat of his heart in her ears, beneath her palm.

"The entangled thread needs to be cut so the thread of divine fate can find its truth," Lorelai said, pulling all their attention.

Calliope let out a sigh as she wiped her eyes.

"But if there's an entangled thread, doesn't that mean, her mate was already divined?" Izzy asked.

Mars shook his head. "The thread never closed. Which means Calliope may have been *his* fate, but—"

"He wasn't hers," Theo spoke solidly.

Mars nodded. "Precisely."

"So how are we going to get this Chuck of the Corn guy to give up his thread *and* the diviner?" Izzy pressed.

Mars huffed in exasperation. "One thing at a time. First, we need to find Chuck."

Calliope met his gaze.

Theo held her close, still not letting go, and Calliope loved the feeling as much as she felt ashamed. Even now, her fingers itched to feel paint and canvas, to paint her aching heart. But they also ached to touch Theo. To get lost in his silken hair, to feel his pulse beneath her palm.

He was her *mate.*

Mars was right, and the moment she'd heard the word, it struck a chord within her, lighting her spark into an eternal flame.

But Chuck had sustained his open thread.

He still believed Calliope was divined to be his. As he had all those years ago.

Perhaps his theft was a desperate attempt to divine his own mate. Or sever the bond that was preventing him from finding his own.

How had things become so complicated?

"And just where are we going to find a pegacorn stalker at?" Izzy asked.

Mars grinned as he gazed back at Lorelai, then at Spike and Izzy. Finally, his softened gaze landed on Calliope and Theodore.

"Why, the only place you'll ever find a horny supernatural on a Monday night. At the *Den of Sin.*"

CHAPTER TEN

IF ONLY TRICK and Shaun could see me now, Theo thought as he stared at the line that was around the block to get into the *Den of Sin.* He'd never been to a *sex club* before. The only experience he'd had remotely close had been the strip club that Trick *insisted* they went to last year when he discovered Theo had never been to one. And he hadn't cared for the experience much. It wasn't anything against the girls, or even the drinks, it just didn't feel right.

Because it wasn't her.

He was starting to understand that all the routes he'd taken had been the wrong ones. But they still led him here... to this ominously designed club with an intimidating line, amidst a vampire, a hellhound, a muse and... whatever the hell Mars was. Theo wasn't certain what his special superpower was.

Though, judging by the way the man was talking to an attendant at the front of the line, he was starting to think Mars's otherworldly ability was talking. Because when he waved them all over, Theo realized they were, indeed, skipping the line. Which made him feel bold and important, but also guilty. How long had those people been standing there?

But he took one look at Calliope, her

dark hair blowing in the air against the setting sun, her eyes dried of the tears she'd shed, though still with faded, smudged eyeliner and mascara and her victory red lipstick, he could not deny she still looked stunning.

Mate.

He'd thought that word the first night he'd met Calliope, felt it in his soul the moment they'd connected. But the idea was whimsical and fantastical because Theodore did not believe in fate or soulmates or bonds forged by unseen forces. Yet, despite his predisposition, he could not seem to stay away from the *muse.*

Muse. That was what Calliope was—a divine being. A *spirit.* A force to inspire and ignite.

Theo could not deny Calliope was

quite an inspiration. For every moment he found himself with her, he felt braver, more confident. He felt powerful and alive. He wanted everything Calliope was willing to give him, and he wanted to give her *everything* he had. His heart, his body, his soul.

Anything you want, Princess.

But Theo could not have Calliope. Not entirely, anyway. Because some winged unicorn had an *open* claim on her. The thought made him angry, jealous, but mostly defensive.

He knew he did not *own* Calliope. He had no claim on her, either. But Theo still felt threatened. The thread was open and this man—pegacorn—had not only stolen the diviner, but as long as his thread remained open, Calliope would never truly be *his*.

And Theo realized, as he followed Calliope and their friends into the *Den of Sin,* that he wanted her to be. His. *Forever.*

But did Calliope want that? Or would Theo be another open thread, left in earnest, only to be severed years from now?

He didn't want to think about such things, so he did the only thing he could. He grabbed Calliope's hand and held it tightly as they walked through the long hallway, into a large room full of activity.

Theo didn't know where to look, or if he even *should* look. There were waiters and waitresses in various states of undress, a stage where a woman was being touched and fondled by two men in various states of bondage and leather. His cheeks heated as he noticed the one man in front of the woman drop to his knees and bury his face in her panties.

"Are you all right?" Calliope asked him.

He squeezed her hand once more. "Just wondering if maybe that spark knocked me out and I'm still laying on the gallery floor," he said, watching as Spike and Izzy swatted at each other playfully. He noticed the way Spike grabbed his vampire girlfriend, the smile on his face. There was a comfort there, as if neither of them truly noticed where they were. When Spike leaned in and kissed her, Theo looked away.

"Theo, I'm sorry, I—"

"It's fine," he lied. "Totally fine. Finding out you're bound to an ancient deity who happens to be tied to a mystical horse who stole a rock from the gallery you work at... just a regular Monday for me."

Calliope swatted his arm. "Mondays truly are the worst."

Theo cracked a smile, if only because he could see the anxiety in her gaze. "They really are."

Mars and Lorelai came to stand in front of them.

"All right, you know the drill. Hang tight, if you see him, signal one of us. Preferably *me*."

Theo nodded. "What... what does he look like?"

Mars shrugged. "You can't miss him. He stands out like a prized pony."

Calliope sighed. "Usually, he wears white. It's an aesthetic thing for him."

Theo looked around the club, noting everyone was in an array of colors, but he didn't see white or ivory anything.

"He's probably either in one of the rooms or he's in the pisser." Mars tutted.

"Rooms?" Theo asked nervously.

"Private rooms. There's plenty of entertainment for you to watch, but for some who prefer a more... private sort of entertainment... Samael has the private rooms. For a fee, of course."

Theo noticed a hallway that was lit up with neon, where it seemed there were far less people. The lights shifted, and for a moment, he thought he saw a flash of lightning, of violet. But it was just a trick of the light.

There was no diviner forging lilac lines or arrows. Just a shadowed hallway lit by neon lights.

"We don't..." Calliope tugged his hand and it was only then he realized they were alone.

Mars and Lorelai had disappeared, and he didn't see Spike or Izzy, either. It was just him and Calliope. Him and his *mate.*

"We don't have to do anything if you don't *want* to. I mean, we're not here for entertainment, we're—"

"It wouldn't be the first time," Theo said with a smirk. "Though, I think I prefer the air of the *DeLux Cafe* better. This is just... a lot."

Calliope nodded, tucking some hair behind her ear. He noticed she seemed a bit nervous, and so he did not think twice about reaching out and pulling her close. She let him, and he did not miss the ease into which she fell into his arms.

"Are you okay?" he asked.

Calliope slid her hands over his chest. She rested her right hand over his heart, imploring him with her amber gaze. "Do you want the truth?" she asked carefully.

Theo nodded, settling his gaze on hers. "Always, Princess."

"No, I am not okay." She shook her head.

He settled his hands on her hips and the sounds of heavy bass thumped around them. He shifted his weight, slowly.

Calliope followed the motion, moving with him.

He slid his hands over her hips carefully, grazing her ass as he pulled her closer.

She leaned into his space, looking up at him, her eyes glassy and warm, searching his for permission. Assurance, perhaps.

Theo did not think twice about giving her what he knew she needed. He leaned in closer, his lips inches away from hers.

"Tell me what you need, Callie," he whispered. "Tell me what you need me to do and I'll do it."

She wrapped her arms around his neck. "I don't know what it is I *need*," she said carefully.

"Then tell me what you *want*." His lips graced hers like a whisper all on their own.

The words were simple, a promise, a prayer. Theo meant them with every ounce of his being. Because she was his *mate*.

Entangled pegacorns and lost McGuffins be damned, she was his divined mate. And there was no denying that when he looked at her underneath the neon lights of the *Den of Sin*, in a crowded room, when all he saw was her. Theo knew it would always be like that. He'd always see her, just as she'd always see him.

"I just want you," she whispered. "And perhaps, a piña colada."

Theo smiled as he caught her gaze. "You can't want something you already have," he murmured, kissing her softly. "I've always been yours. From the moment I stepped into the DeLux Cafe."

Her fingernails teased the edges of his hair. She leaned up on her toes, kissing him once more, pulling him into her.

Her kiss was pure magic. Kissing Calliope felt like an out of body experience and Theo didn't want it to ever end.

She pulled away, following his motions, and they danced together, unaware of the sex and debauchery taking place around them. As far as they were concerned, there was only *this*. The muse and her masterpiece.

"Theo..." She barely got his name out before his lips were on hers again, his cock stiffening in his jeans as her hands slid down his sides.

She pulled him closer and he followed her without hesitation.

And then he *felt* it. The undeniable tug in his chest, the energy that always seemed to fester between them. It reared its head like a spirit of its own making and he clutched his chest.

Calliope stopped, holding him still. "Theo..."

CALLIOPE

He looked up, noting the violet lines of energy traveling, traipsing through the room. Theo did not think twice. For he knew precisely what this energy, this fractal of circumstance was.

And so Theo ran, as fast as he could, through the crowd, through the sweat and the shadows, chasing the light, Calliope hot on his tail.

CHAPTER ELEVEN

EVERYTHING HAD HAPPENED so quickly, Calliope barely had time to ascertain it all. One moment she was kissing Theo as he declared his devotion for her once more, and the next, he was chasing divining light across the room.

Her heels clacked on the floor as she sprinted toward him, Isabelle and Spike's voices calling out to her. But it was Mars's voice she responded to.

"The lights are shining!" she called

out, chasing Theo through the crowd until she'd come to a stage on the other side of the room.

His wings were the first thing she saw. Outstretched beyond the wingback chair he had settled in. No, the *throne* he had settled in. On stage, a woman performed, kneeling before a man wearing a dark, tailored suit.

Theo stopped just shy of the chair, and Calliope could see the faint violet energy circling the chair.

"Chuck," Mars called, and Calliope froze.

She could not tear her gaze from Theo and Mars, nor could she tear it from *Pegasus.*

He turned in his chair, his bright blue eyes catching her gaze. Soft, golden blond hair fell in his eyes, covering the illuminating glowing horn on his head, and he looked no different than the last time she'd seen him. Timeless. Angelic. He was decked out in his usual white suit with gold accoutrements, his wings spread out and large, like a threat.

"Mars, how good to see you." His voice was smooth, carrying that air of cockiness that grated on Calliope's nerves.

"Calliope..." He looked up at her, pinning her to her spot. His smile was faint, a ghost of one, if any.

But it was his eyes, full of ache and pain and fear, that resonated with her. They were not the eyes of the man she remembered. The one who loved himself above all else.

"Chuck," she swallowed sharply as all the memories came flooding back.

The good and the bad.

He looked Theo up and down as Isabelle, Spike, and Lorelai flanked her side.

"Who are you?" Chuck asked.

Theo took a step forward. "I am Calliope's mate."

His truth was her spark, and the moment he said it, she felt the energy between them grow. Lines of violet energy culminated around Chuck's throne from where he sat it and she could not help but move. She knew the truth, and there was no more denying it.

Chuck scoffed. "Oh, Callie, sweetheart, don't tell me this is what you're into now." He looked at Theo with an annoyed glare. As if Theo was not a human, and certainly not worthy of being her mate.

"What I prefer is none of your business, Chuck," she said as she took her strides toward the man.

Chuck rose, and the sight made her stop. His wings did not fold. He kept them open, if only to appear menacing.

"You have something that belongs to Callie," Mars said, flanking the pegacorn's left side.

Chuck turned to raise an eyebrow at Mars. "Oh, is this how it is now? I call you and you don't answer, but if *Calliope* calls, you suddenly have time to see *her*?"

Calliope stepped forth. "This is not a game, Chuck. It is my *life*."

Theo wrapped his arm around her waist.

Chuck shook his head, his feathers tinkling like chimes as they stretched from his motion.

"Of course it is a game!" he bit. "It's always a game with you, Calliope. Except you are always changing the rules. It is exhausting."

Theo stepped forth. "You have no claim here, Chuck E. Cheese," he bit. "Your thread is *open*. Callie doesn't want you. Please, let her go and give us the diviner."

Chuck snarled at them. "And you think she wants *you*? Oh, how tragic."

Theo growled and Calliope noted the faint purple energy surrounding Theodore.

Chuck stopped in front of Theo.

Mars stood beside his right side as Spike flanked his left.

"Give the diviner back," she said solidly. "I know you have it, I can see the threads emanating around you."

Chuck crossed his arms. "No."

Mars advanced on his friend. "Chuck, come on, don't do this…"

Chuck snapped at him. "Do not pretend to care now, Mars! You have no idea what I have been through, what I—"

"You do not need to hold Calliope's fate hostage," Spike called. "The diviner won't make her love you."

Chuck laughed and Calliope felt tears prickle her eyes.

"I don't want *her* love," Chuck growled.

The light of the stage lit him up, making him look like a devil in white.

Theo closed the gap between him and Chuck. "Then it shouldn't be so hard to let her go," he said through his teeth.

"You fools, I don't want the muse,"

Chuck bit. "I want my *mate.*"

"Then let me go, Chuck. Sever this thread so we can both be free," Calliope said through a choked sob.

"I can't!" Chuck hissed. He slid his hand in his pocket, and Calliope gasped as he brought out the diviner. He held it in his hand like it was nothing more than a crystal, as if it did not hold fate in its core.

"Chuck, put the diviner down," Mars said cautiously. "Take a breath. Let's talk about this."

Calliope noted Chuck's eyes blaze bright, cerulean. He was close to shifting, and she knew such a thing could be dangerous in a room full of people. Because when Chuck shifted into his true form, his light would blind those who could not stand the sight.

Humans.

And the *Den of Sin* was packed with them tonight.

Chuck's wings bristled. "Talk? Since when does Mars, the God of fucking *War* talk?"

Theo moved closer, but Calliope pushed him back.

"Theo, I need you to turn around and—"

"I am not going anywhere, Callie. Not now, not ever."

Calliope did not have time to argue. She could not think, she could only act on impulse. The spark inside of her warmed as Theo held her close, and the room heated. Violet light surrounded Chuck, his blue eyes flickering to white and lilac.

"Chucky, seriously. I know you're

frustrated, but you're in the *Den*, there's people here, you can't—"

"You think I don't know that!" Chuck yelled. He gripped the diviner tight and Spike cursed as Lorelai and Izzy called out for him to put the diviner down. Bright light poured through the cracks of his fist.

"I came here with this bloody fucking stone that's supposed to work, but it doesn't fucking work!" Chuck yelled, his body now shaking. His wings fluttered, and a crowd was starting to form.

"It doesn't work, Chuck, because you can't force love!" Calliope bellowed.

She pushed Theodore aside as she took two strides toward the pegacorn on the verge of a shift.

Perhaps it was foolish and dangerous, but Calliope knew what Chuck—what

Pegasus—needed. She always knew what her *patrons* needed. Because they were her patrons, not her friends or her family or the loves of her lives.

"The diviner forces it all the time," he snarled. "That is why it was created, Calliope. You know that. You were *there.*"

Her heart slowed at his words. She did know. She knew when the diviners were forged, how important they would be for the gods and supernaturals alike. No more needless deaths or heartbreak. Love would be as simple as touching the stone and following the light.

But the years went by and buried the diviners, and gods and goddesses and supernatural shifters and monsters and every other creature had faded to chasing destiny on their own. Making their mistakes, their choices, their masterpieces all on their own.

Without a silly rock.

"I was there," she bit, staring up at Chuck's glowing eyes. "And so were *you,*" she said, tears pooling in her eyes. "You can not force the hand of fate, Pegasus. You must let fate take its course."

Chuck crushed the stone in his hand and Calliope gasped as she watched the debris slip through his fingers.

"Pegasus..." she breathed his name, his true name, as the lights in the room started to cut out.

Chuck's shoulders shook as Calliope dropped to the ground, reaching for the debris, the broken pieces of the diviner.

"No..." she cried, the tears falling like rain. Diviner dust slipped through her fingers.

"What have you done?" she asked. She stood, the diviner debris slipping through her fingers and her spark ignited. Passion, anger, guilt, sadness... it all caught like fire on dry leaves.

She lunged for Chuck, and moments later, she felt Mars at her side, grabbing the shifter as Spike grabbed the other side. Between Mars and Spike, Chuck thrashed, hissing, snarling growling, and then Calliope saw the tears.

Streaming down Chuck's angelic face. She saw his grimace of pain, heard it in his voice.

"Fate forced my hand," he cried. "And now I am alone."

Mars and Spike held him but he stopped thrashing.

"Fate is not real," Chuck snapped, his voice edged with anger and pain, but not just any pain. Pain of *loss*. And it was at that precise moment, that Calliope understood the man she knew had changed.

He'd loved. And he'd lost.

His lover, his friend. His sense of self.

And in that loss he turned desperate, aching for the love those he loved had discovered on their own.

Calliope gasped at this realization, her eyes going wide as she stared up at Chuck's glowing, sad eyes.

But it was Theo who stepped forth.

CHAPTER TWELVE

THEO LOOKED CHUCK in the eyes sternly. "No, you're wrong."

Chuck shoved off Mars and Spike, lunging forward. He hissed at Theo, but Theo did not back down.

"You know nothing," Chuck sneered. "You are a human. You can not understand."

"But I do," Theo said carefully. He recognized the anger, the guilt in Chuck's eyes. He'd seen it in his own reflection time and time again.

"I did not believe in fate or destiny or preconceived notions. I thought fate could not be real because if it was, it was a fucking dick." Theo pursed his lips. "Fate took from me, too."

Chuck snarled as he got in Theo's face, but Theo still did not back down. The energy he'd felt next to Calliope was everywhere now. Around him, inside of him.

And so he channeled it, he used it to fuel him.

"And then my roommate forced me to go to this stupid masquerade and..." He turned to look at Calliope. His mate.

She knelt on the floor, divine dust in her hands, slipping like the sands of an hourglass.

Chuck had destroyed the diviner. But

in Theo's heart, he knew the magic was not within the diviner itself. It was like many things, in the belief.

Theo did not believe in fate, but he did believe in the power between hearts, between palms, between souls.

And perhaps, that was enough for Theodore. Eternal bonds or not, he believed in the energy, the love that existed between him and a woman. A muse.

"Then I met Callie, and that changed. I changed."

Chuck hissed at him. "Fool. That is what she does. She is like a spider, sneaking into your ear and laying eggs until one day they hatch and when they are gone, you are not the same."

Theo shook his head. "Fate may not be real, but you are." The two of them stood there in the light, like the sun and moon.

Theo was aware in his peripheral vision, Spike and Mars were waiting, guarded. Ready to jump in should the tide turn. Isabelle and Lorelai flanked Calliope, who was crying.

Theo hated to hear his *mate* cry.

"You can change your fate," he said. "You just have to let go of what's holding you *back*."

Theo turned to look at Calliope, her eyes red rimmed. He hadn't understood before. He was angry, too. And that anger, that pain—the baggage he'd carried for his ex-fiancé and his failed relationships, his embarrassment and guilt over his sensitive cock, his own self-loathing... it was all holding him back from what he wanted more than anything.

Love.

And the moment he'd let go, the moment he left the choice up to fate, he'd found Calliope. In a bar, drinking pomegranate martinis.

Chuck reached one hand out and wrapped it around Theo's throat, his anger boiling over. Mars and Spike tried to separate them, but it was no use. Theo coughed, unable to breathe, and in his last attempt to be reasonable, he reached out and grabbed Chuck's neck, and the world faded into lilac.

The *Den of Sin* disappeared, and all there was, was the nothing. And the faint sound of laughter. Calliope's laughter.

And then he saw it. Calliope in her youth, dark hair framing her face in curls, wearing a toga. She looked different, but the eyes... those were the same deep amber eyes he'd come to know and love.

And the man with her, a young Pegasus. Laughing, carefree.

But laughter turned to arguments, and arguments turned to darkness, and darkness turned to armor. To self-preservation. Theo watched a great god become a shell of himself. A man portraying greatness when inside, he felt empty and void of love.

And then he'd watched all the women come and go. He'd watched a man laugh and drink, sharing in camaraderie with his friend. Mars.

He watched Chuck try to reach out to Calliope, only to be ignored. Watched him force a mask of bravery for his friend who was dying, watched as that friend slipped through his fingers like divining dust.

And he watched a crying, desperate Chuck transform into a beautiful white unicorn and break the glass.

His desperation was heartbreaking. And Theo understood.

The images faded into shadow until all there was, was light. And so Theodore chased the light, until he found the man it was emanating from.

Theo reached out for the man, offering him his hand.

"You're not alone," he said.

The man, thin and pale, looked scared. His blue eyes were dull and his hair, not shiny or well kept. His horn glinted off the light emanating from between them.

"But you're never going to find what you want unless you let go of the past and let someone else *in*."

The man fixed his gaze on Theo. "You just want me to let go of her so you can have her. You just want to take the last bond I have left because you want her for yourself."

Theo sighed. "I came here because of that, yes. But that's not why I'm here, now."

The feeling of despair and pain and loathing pervaded in the space. And Theo knew exactly what he needed to do. Because it had been done for him, twice.

Once when Trick took him under his wing, and once when a hellhound drove him home.

So, Theodore Lange held his hand out to the bitter pegacorn.

"Hi, my name's Theodore. Like the chipmunk. But you can call me Theo."

Chuck looked at his hand as if it were a snake. But Theo did not remove it. He kept it still in the space between them.

Chuck looked at him, then his hand. And then Theo felt the warmth of Chuck's hand in his.

"Name's Pegasus. But everyone calls me Chuck."

Theo smiled and shook his hand. "Nice to meet you, Chuck."

And just like that, the world dissipated into reality once more, and Theo blinked, noting Mars, Lorelai, Spike, Izzy, and Calliope were hovering over him... and Pegasus—er, Chuck— along with many other people.

For the second time that night, he sat up, and Spike held his shoulder. "Easy, you two took a fucking fall."

Chuck groaned beside him as Mars helped him up, squeezing his shoulder.

"You all right there, Chucky?" Mars asked, the concern evident in his voice.

Theo noticed how Chuck looked different. His eyebrows were furrowed, his expression softer.

"What happened?" he asked, and even his voice was different.

"Theo knocked you out with his superpowers, obviously," Izzy murmured.

Chuck looked at Theo, his blue eyes sparkling with something that wasn't there before.

Hope.

"Theo..." he said Theo's name, and it was not harsh, but rather as if he was truly hearing it for the first time.

Calliope's gasp pulled all their attention.

Theo lunged forward, grasping for Calliope, needing to feel her in his arms.

"Theo, look," she whispered, and it took Theo far too long to actually look because he was too caught up in her scent, her hair, her flesh, her mouth...

And then he saw it.

The diviner in her hands. Fusing back together, like magnets.

Until it was once again whole.

"I thought he broke it," Lorelai said, clutching close to Mars.

"He did," Izzy said in wonder.

"He broke the thread," Mars murmured. "And in turn, he broke the hold it had on him."

Calliope choked, sniffling as tears fell down her face.

"I don't know what you guys are talking about, why is everyone crying?" Chuck asked.

Theo clapped him on the back, while holding Calliope close. "It's a long story, but, uh... maybe we can talk about it tomorrow? I'm kind of exhausted after all of that."

"Me too," Spike said.

"I am going to third that and say yes, let's get the fuck out of here," Izzy chimed.

Lorelai smiled. "And get that diviner back where it belongs."

Calliope sniffled again and Theo grinned as he noticed the small thread, jutting out of his chest, landing against Calliope's.

The diviner didn't lie.

Calliope was his soul mate.

But he didn't need a rock to tell him such.

All he needed was to look in her eyes.

"And it is a school night," Theo said with a smirk.

Calliope laughed through her tears.

CHAPTER THIRTEEN

WHEN THEO PULLED the car up to her apartment, neither of them moved, even after the car had been turned off.

They sat in companionable silence, processing the events of the night. Well, perhaps, the last few *days*, if Calliope was being honest.

"Can I walk you to your door?" Theo asked, turning to look at her.

The diviner was gone, nestled back in the gallery, but this time, Calliope had chosen to secure it in the vault in the office. While Pegasus seemed to be not as irritable and angry, she didn't want to take chances. Though Theo seemed to think whatever had happened had indeed worked. He wouldn't call it magic, but Calliope knew magic was most certainly involved. But she did not press Theo, instead she leaned back, closed her eyes and listened to the radio as her *mate* drove her home.

"I'd like that," she said with a smile as he got out of the car to open her door.

He offered her his hand, and she took it without question. Suddenly, everything made sense. Her apprehension, her anger toward Chuck. Her reluctance to see him. The thread between them needed to be cut. It had affected them both, and now that it was severed, she was free to be with her true divine mate.

Theodore Lange.

Who stood in the face of an angry ex-boyfriend pegacorn and offered him *friendship*.

It was not the vampire or the hellhound, or the God of War, or the muse herself that had saved them all—including the patrons of the *Den of Sin*—from a blinding monster. It was the *human*.

It was Theodore and his heart. The very heart that loved her and challenged her and inspired her.

He truly was her Zorro, sword and all, saving the day.

She reached for his hand as they walked up her sidewalk and her steps. And when he'd reached her porch, he leaned to kiss her and she did not fight it.

She grasped his neck with her hand, kissing him adamantly, with all her might. And just like before, his kiss was perfect. Slow and steady but also warm and seductive and commanding all at once.

He broke away, a faint smile on his face. "I love you," he said, his voice as steady as a river.

Calliope's chest warmed and her spark lit up like a firework all throughout her being. Because she knew his words were true.

"I love you, too," she said sweetly. "I know it feels odd but... nothing's ever felt more right."

Theo smiled, leaning his forehead against hers. "Good night, Princess," he said, and just as he turned to leave, she grasped his wrist.

"Stay."

That one word was more freeing than it should have been. Calliope smiled because it felt right, too. She did want Theo to stay. Now and forever.

She tugged Theo by the hand, and he followed without protest.

"Are you sure?" he asked.

Calliope nodded. *"Oui."*

Theo grinned, his shy, sweet demeanor fading once more, giving way to the seductive, alluring Theo Calliope only wanted to see more of.

She pulled him through her front door, before locking it and turning the lights on. It was strange to think they'd been here not so long ago, but somehow everything was different. They were different.

Calliope smiled as she pulled him close, kissing him slowly.

Theo reciprocated, kissing her back with adamant fervor.

She removed his shirt first, and he worked at the buttons on her jacket. Her hands made quick work of unbuttoning his jeans, and they leisurely ambled through the living room into her bedroom, discarding their clothes as they went. They were in their underwear within ten minutes, and had collapsed on the bed nearly instantly.

Theo kissed her reverently. His mouth traveled down her ear to her jaw, to her neck as he pulled her close, spooning her from behind.

Calliope settled into his space as he held her close, burying his face in her hair. He breathed her in and the sound was sweeter than any bell.

His arm slid across her waist, settling over her stomach. His fingers tickled the edges of her panties and she closed her eyes, backing herself up against his cock, smiling when she realized he was already hard and ready.

She wiggled her ass against him as he groaned into her shoulder.

"Do you want to cuddle?" she asked sweetly.

"Cuddling is good. I like cuddling."

Calliope giggled.

"*Voulez-vous coucher avec moi, ce soir?*" he asked, his voice quite serious.

"*Oui,*" she said as she wiggled her ass again against his cock.

Theo let out a deep sigh. "Cuddle fuck then? Meet in the middle?" he asked, his voice tinged with laughter.

But before Calliope could fully answer, Theo had upended her onto her back and was already removing her panties. She watched him, noting the way he moved, the way he carefully touched her, stroked her.

"This doesn't look like cuddling," she pouted, but when Theodore found his home between her legs, his tongue and fingers buried inside her, she forgot mostly everything else.

Her hand found his hair and she tightened her grip as his tongue swiped along her sensitive folds before he slipped two fingers inside her. She ground herself against his torturous fingers and tongue until she was writhing in ecstasy. And then she'd pushed Theo over onto his back, taking his cock into her mouth in one swift motion. A few sucks and licks, and he was a goner, moaning out his release as his eyes fell shut. When they were spent, he wrapped his arm around her once more under the covers, his cock pressed to her seam.

A moment later, she felt him breaching her entrance, and her eyes started to flutter shut.

Theo peppered her neck and jaw with kisses, his cock sliding in easily to her soaked pussy.

Calliope lost herself in the ecstasy. Theo's slow, smooth strokes were like a lullaby.

"All yours, Calliope," he whispered as he kissed her ear, thrusting into her, filling her with his release. He did not cry or whimper, but instead, he sighed a sound of deep contentment.

Calliope pushed back against him, relishing in the feel of his warmth ricocheting through her, and her orgasm hit her.

She moaned softly as he held her tight. "All yours, Theodore.

The slumber took them like thieves in a gallery, their hearts beating as one, both of them drifting off, the dawn of a new day on the horizon. And as the sun rose, bathing Calliope's bedroom in shades of ochre and cadmium, Calliope and Theo found their inspiration once more in each other's arms.

Thank you for reading Calliope!

If you enjoyed this book, please return to the retailer and leave a review. Your words mean so much and help us to continue writing the books you love.

Follow our Facebook page
Speed Dating with the Denizens of the Underworld Series

Watch your favorite online retailer for the other books in the Speed Dating with the Denizens of the Underworld series.

Watch for the other books in the
Speed Dating with the Denizens of the
Underworld Series

Lucifer

Hecate

Demi

Hades

Orion

Hera

Triton

Athena

Zeus

Medusa

Spike

Calliope

Artemis

And More!

OTHER BOOKS BY ARIEL DAWN

The Hunter Games

Blood Of My Enemy

Blood Of The Lost

Thorne Of Blood

Speed Dating with the Denizens of the Underworld Series

Hecate

Hades

Orion

Athena

Spike

Calliope

The Forevermore Series

In The Cards

In The Shadows

In The Deep

In The Night

Shifters Of Starfall Creek Series

Hollow's Sunrise

Hollow's Sunset

Hollow's Legacy

Shifters of Starfall Creek Collection:

Books 1-3

Sign up for Ariel Dawn's newsletter and claim your sweet treat!

https://view.flodesk.com/pages/64b2b6

efe181ddda00ff2a1e

CONNECT WITH ARIEL DAWN

Website

http://www.ariel-dawn.com/

Goodreads:

http://www.goodreads.com/authorariel

dawn

Bookbub:

http://www.bookbub.com/authors/ariel

-dawn

Facebook:

http://www.facebook.com/authorarielda

wn

Twitter:

https://twitter.com/ArielDawn10

Join Dusk Chasers—Ariel Dawn's Official Readers Group for access to exclusive content!

https://www.facebook.com/groups/689167388350361

ABOUT ARIEL DAWN

USA TODAY BESTSELLING AUTHOR Ariel Dawn grew up as an avid reader and is a creative soul.
What started out as writing reviews for indie romance authors led to featuring quirky, stereotypical, and weird covers on her Instagram Wrong Turn Romance, which gave her the courage to finally decide to live her dream and become an author.
Ariel writes plot driven paranormal romance and hopes to venture into fantasy and rom-com in the future. When she isn't writing, she can be found cosplaying, attending conventions, creating all sorts of artwork in her studio, or editing photos for her photography business.
A self-professed geek and foodie, she loves hanging out with family and friends and playing video games and board games with her retro gamer husband.